Sister Act

"Gardner and his gang held up a military payroll detail, murdered six men and the payroll officer, and escaped with more than thirty thousand dollars, almost all of it in coin." Hard money, most of it silver, was the normal method of payment for the military.

Longarm whistled softly. "Thirty thousand. That's a right tidy haul, Boss."

"So it is. Five or six thousand a man, the way I hear it. Of course that was almost a year ago. There is no telling where those gang members are now." The chief marshal smiled. "Except for Gardner himself. Some very helpful someone took him into custody down south and there he sits, waiting for you to come fetch him home for trial." Billy's expression hardened. "And hanging. He will surely swing for killing all those soldiers."

"This happened in our district?" Longarm asked.

"Just south of Fort Caspar. Gardner and his people set an ambush, apparently a rather clever one, at a ford across a very small creek. The men disguised themselves as nuns in need of assistance. Which of course the payroll officer was quick to offer. The next thing you knew those 'nuns' had produced sawed-off shotguns and had everyone controlled. The coldhearted bastards tied the soldiers' hands, lined them up, and shot them down, no mercy given whatsoever. You can see why we want this man to hang."

→► **TABOR EVANS** ◄←

LONGARM

AND THE 400 BLOWS

J

JOVE BOOKS, NEW YORK

THE BERKLEY PUBLISHING GROUP
Published by the Penguin Group
Penguin Group (USA) Inc.
375 Hudson Street, New York, New York 10014, USA
Penguin Group (Canada), 90 Eglinton Avenue East, Suite 700, Toronto, Ontario M4P 2Y3, Canada
(a division of Pearson Penguin Canada Inc.)
Penguin Books Ltd., 80 Strand, London WC2R 0RL, England
Penguin Group Ireland, 25 St. Stephen's Green, Dublin 2, Ireland (a division of Penguin Books Ltd.)
Penguin Group (Australia), 250 Camberwell Road, Camberwell, Victoria 3124, Australia
(a division of Pearson Australia Group Pty. Ltd.)
Penguin Books India Pvt. Ltd., 11 Community Centre, Panchsheel Park, New Delhi—110 017, India
Penguin Group (NZ), 67 Apollo Drive, Rosedale, Auckland 0632, New Zealand
(a division of Pearson New Zealand Ltd.)
Penguin Books (South Africa) (Pty.) Ltd., 24 Sturdee Avenue, Rosebank, Johannesburg 2196,
South Africa

Penguin Books Ltd., Registered Offices: 80 Strand, London WC2R 0RL, England

This is a work of fiction. Names, characters, places, and incidents either are the product of the author's imagination or are used fictitiously, and any resemblance to actual persons, living or dead, business establishments, events, or locales is entirely coincidental

LONGARM AND THE 400 BLOWS

A Jove Book / published by arrangement with the author

PRINTING HISTORY
Jove edition / March 2012

Copyright © 2012 by Penguin Group (USA) Inc.
Cover illustration by Milo Sinovcic.

ISBN: 978-0-515-15047-6

JOVE®
Jove Books are published by The Berkley Publishing Group,
a division of Penguin Group (USA) Inc.,
375 Hudson Street, New York, New York 10014.
JOVE® is a registered trademark of Penguin Group (USA) Inc.
The "J" design is a trademark of Penguin Group (USA) Inc.

PRINTED IN THE UNITED STATES OF AMERICA

10 9 8 7 6 5 4 3 2 1

Chapter 1

His hand snaked blindly out from beneath the covers and fumbled for the bulbous Ingersoll pocket watch he always kept within reach on the bedside table. Except . . . he could not find it. In fact could not find the bedside table.

His eyes came open. Reluctantly. And painfully. He winced at the bright daylight streaming in past the blinds, light that was coming from the wrong side of his room.

His head throbbed and his mouth felt like it had been filled with cotton. Dirty cotton at that.

He must have really tied one on last night, he concluded. It was all the fault of that wine. If he had been drinking his usual rye whiskey, he surely would not have a head like this. But she ordered wine instead and . . .

Whoa! She. What *she*?

Deputy United States Marshal Custis Long became aware of a warm presence pressed against his hip. And of the fact that he was *not* in his own bed here.

Lordy, what . . . ?

He rolled his head to the side, sharp pains stabbing his

eyeballs and pounding the inside of his skull, and blinked back the stickiness that pasted layers of glue on his eyelids.

He saw a mass of blond curls beside his shoulder. Became aware of the flowery scent of a perfume or a powder. Noticed a pale, rubbery tit peering out from beneath the sheet that covered both he and . . . and whoever the woman was. Try as he might, he could not remember who the hell she was or what she looked like.

He sure must have liked the look of her last night though. That thought brought a small smile. Damn that wine, though. He could not remember a thing about the evening.

Well, not much of it anyway.

He did remember something about being thrown out of Nate Kelley's Bar and Grill and laughing about it at the time. He remembered that the blond woman—what the *hell* was her name anyway?—had a laugh that sounded like a mule braying.

But she had great tits. He remembered that well enough. Big tits.

He rolled a little further onto his side so he could reach over and take hold of the one that was exposed. It was soft. Doughy. As flaccid as his dick was right now.

The woman snorted in her sleep and turned onto her back, exposing the other tit, too. She had nipples as big as most women have tits. And her tits were rather ugly, criss-crossed with blue veins lying just under the skin.

She turned her head a little and started to snore. He could see her face now. Wished she had continued to look the other way. She was . . . not pretty. It would have been uncharitable to say that the woman was ugly. But . . . she was ugly. That was the long and the short of it. This bed partner was just plain butt ugly.

Longarm carefully, very carefully, extricated himself

from her touch and from her bed. He stood, well over six feet tall and sturdy with broad shoulders, narrow hips, and powerful—if currently quite naked—legs.

He had brown hair and a broad, full sweep of mustache, a face more craggy than handsome, and soft eyes that could turn hard as flint when the occasion demanded. For reasons he himself did not understand, women tended to find him handsome while men generally thought him trustworthy.

Now he eased away from the side of the bed and found a velvet-covered dressing table chair to perch on while he silently dressed in brown corduroy trousers, a calfskin vest, black stovepipe cavalry boots, a brown tweed coat, and a snuff-brown, flat-crowned Stetson hat.

His final, and most necessary, piece of apparel was a black gun belt that placed his double-action .45-caliber Colt revolver in a cross-draw rig.

The errant Ingersoll he discovered on the blond woman's dressing table. The watch went into the appropriate vest pocket with its chain extending across the flat of his belly to the other pocket where it ended in a .41-caliber derringer that was attached to his watch chain. The little pistol had come in mighty handy a time or two in the past.

Longarm tucked watch and pistol into his vest pockets and tiptoed out into the hallway of what appeared to be a rather run-down hotel.

My, oh my, how had he come to be here?

Once he was safely out of the woman's room he smiled. From the feel of things, throbbing head and cotton mouth and all, he must have had a helluva fine night of it.

Yes, sir, he must really have enjoyed himself.

Time now to get to work, though.

Chapter 2

"You're late," Chief Marshal Vail's clerk Henry accused from behind his desk.

Longarm hung his Stetson on the hat rack in the corner of the outer office and turned, grinning. "Yeah, but if I know you, old hoss, you was here an hour early this morning." He held his hands out, one high and one low, and slowly brought them side by side. "Between us we balance out," he said, grinning.

"The boss might not think so," Henry said, light reflecting off his spectacles and making his eyes invisible behind the glare. "He's been looking for you."

"Shit," Longarm grumbled. Most mornings it did not much matter if he was a wee bit late. Or, as in this case, an hour and a half late.

He crossed to the door leading into Chief U.S. Marshal William Vail's private office and politely tapped on it.

"Come in," a voice called from inside.

Longarm opened the door and stepped in.

"You," Billy Vail said, his tone suggesting the word was more accusation than greeting.

"Good morning, Boss," Longarm said contritely.

"I suppose you have a good explanation," the pink-cheeked, almost entirely bald marshal said. The man looked like he should have been in the outer office working as a clerk, looked mild mannered and gentle. In truth he was a former Texas Ranger who was as salty as the worst of the desperadoes he once chased.

"No, sir. No excuse, sir," Longarm said, straightening to a rather ragged form of attention.

"Well, that is a surprise anyway." Billy waved a hand dismissively. "I suppose the truth is that you were engaged in some sort of debauchery with a trollop. Or worse. In which case I would rather not know about it."

The marshal sniffed once, then leaned forward to sort through a slim sheaf of papers laid out on his desk. He found the one he wanted and extracted it from the pile, leaning back in his swivel armchair and peering across the desk at Deputy Custis Long.

"I have a job for you," Billy announced.

"Yes, sir?" Not that the information was any great surprise. Why the hell else would Billy call him in here except to give him an assignment? Well, either that or to fire him. Or threaten to. Or . . . In retrospect perhaps there were a great many reasons why Longarm might now be standing at attention in front of Billy's desk.

Vail turned the sheet of paper—it was a bright yellow Western Union message form—around to face Longarm and pushed it across the desk to him.

"May I?" Longarm picked up the telegram and took a look.

HOLDING ANTON GARDNER FORT MARION **STOP**
YOU TRANSPORT FOR TRIAL DENVER DISTRICT **STOP**
ADVISE EARLIEST **STOP** S/ CRAIG

"The name Gardner I recognize," Longarm said. "Fort Marion I don't. Where would that be?"

"Don't feel bad about not recognizing it," Billy said. "I had to look it up myself. It's on the Atlantic coast somewhere south of Jacksonville, Florida. An old Spanish fort, I understand. I knew the name but not where it is."

"Oh, hell. O' course. They been holding a bunch of renegade Injuns there."

"Off and on," Billy said, nodding.

"Who is this Craig who signed the telegram?"

Vail shrugged. "The marshal for that district perhaps or the army officer in charge of the fort. I really don't know, but I'm sure you will find out when you get there."

"When I get there," Longarm repeated.

"Exactly. I want you to go there—there will be no need for extradition papers since Gardner is already in the custody of the United States government—secure the prisoner and transport him back here for trial."

"I recognize the name, Billy, but what'd he do exactly?"

"Gardner and his gang held up a military payroll detail, murdered six men and the payroll officer, and escaped with more than thirty thousand dollars, almost all of it in coin." Hard money, most of it silver, was the normal method of payment for the military.

Longarm whistled softly. "Thirty thousand. That's a right tidy haul, Boss."

"So it is. Five or six thousand a man, the way I hear it. Of course that was almost a year ago. There is no telling where those gang members are now." He smiled. "Except for Gardner himself. Some very helpful someone took him into custody down south and there he sits, waiting for you to come fetch him home for trial." Billy's expression hardened. "And hanging. He will surely swing for killing all those soldiers."

"This happened in our district?" Longarm asked.

"Just south of Fort Caspar. Gardner and his people set an ambush, apparently a rather clever one, at a ford across a very small creek. The men disguised themselves as nuns in need of assistance. Which of course the payroll officer was quick to offer. The next thing you knew, those 'nuns' had produced sawed-off shotguns and had everyone controlled. The coldhearted bastards tied the soldiers' hands, lined them up, and shot them down, no mercy given whatsoever. You can see why we want this man to hang."

"Damn right. What about the rest of the gang?"

Billy shrugged. "We have no idea who they are. Or I suppose I should say 'were.' It is unlikely they would still be together. Not after this much time and that much money divided among them. The only reason we know anything about what happened up there is because of sign left behind on the ground and the nuns', um, they call those black things 'habits,' don't they?"

"I believe they do, yes, sir."

"They left the habits behind. And their empty shotgun shells. The bastards!" Billy scowled and pushed more papers across the desk to Longarm. "Anyway, here are your orders for Gardner. You can get the usual travel vouchers, rather more of them than usual I should think, from Henry."

"One thing, Boss. Any idea how I go about gettin' to this Fort Marion place?"

Billy laughed. "Not a clue, Longarm. Not one single clue. But I have every confidence that you will find it. And that you will bring Anton Gardner back here to face trial and hanging."

"Yes, sir. I figure t' do just that. The whole deal sounds long an' boring but easy enough."

He had been wrong about such things before, too.

Chapter 3

A long journey, had he said? He hadn't known the half of it. The damn trip was going to take more than a week. And that was just to *get* there! Trains, ferries, who the hell knew what else. Longarm fervently wished the boss had chosen to send someone else on this boring journey, but everyone except for the new kid was already assigned work and this was simply too long a jaunt—and Anton Gardner too mean a son of a bitch—to trust to a newcomer like the kid.

Longarm sighed and accepted his fate. Fort Marion, the boss had said, so Fort Marion it would be. If he could just figure out how to get there.

He could go north to Julesburg and east on the Union Pacific from there. But that would dump him off in the middle of the country with the choice of taking a ferry across the river, another train to Chicago and who the hell knew from there.

He could travel all the way down to Texas and then east, but railroads were spotty down that way. There were plenty of them but they were mostly short-line outfits that may or may not connect with something else going in the direction he needed.

After consultation with half a dozen different maps and three separate ticket clerks at two different Denver railroad terminals, Longarm finally decided to take the long familiar Denver and Rio Grande south to Pueblo, the Kansas and Pacific for his first leg east, ferry across the Mississippi to Memphis and from there down through Atlanta to . . . he wasn't sure. From there he would go either to Savannah or down to Jacksonville. After that it would be either a stagecoach or a coastal steamer to get farther south to St. Augustine and Fort Marion.

It seemed a miserable damned trip just for one prisoner. As far as Longarm was concerned they could hang the piece of shit there and save everyone—himself among them—a whole hell of a lot of trouble.

Still, that decision was not his to make. He was just a foot soldier in this process. Billy Vail and the Department of Justice were the generals.

Grumbling every step of the way, Longarm returned to his boardinghouse and packed a second bag in addition to the one he usually carried. No saddle or carbine this time out though. That would help minimize the crap he had to drag along.

He remembered to include a set of leg irons. With a prick like Gardner handcuffs might not be enough.

And shirts. Of course. Balbriggans. Dressy striped trousers instead of his usual rough corduroys. Collars. Of course. He was likely to need a goodly number of celluloid collars. Spare collar buttons. A razor and shaving soap because there might or might not be opportunity to visit a barber along the way. Bar soap and a hand towel since he had no idea what sort of accommodations might be available.

Shit, he hated this nuisance.

Okay, what he really hated was the fact that Oliphant's Traveling Troupe would be long gone from Denver by the time he got back, and there was a honey of a dancer in the chorus line that he had been softening up for the last few days.

Just a little while longer and he was certain he would get a look at what she hid under her skirt. Perhaps much more than merely a look.

Now, damnit, she would be off to Nevada or California or some damn place by the time he got home.

Still, duty called.

Longarm remembered to pack extra cartridges for his .45. A full box of them.

Just in case.

Then he toted his carpetbag plus a Gladstone out to the street and whistled up a hackney to take him to the D&RG depot.

Chapter 4

By the time he stepped off the train in Atlanta, Longarm felt pretty much like shit, gritty and ragged and out of sorts. He needed a bath and a shave and a good night's sleep.

He had tried to shave on the train but only succeeded in cutting himself thanks to the jolting and bumping of one damned train after another. He tried to wash himself but found soot and specks of cinder in the water given to him for the purpose. He tried to sleep but was continually bumped and jostled by other passengers crowded into the railroad coach.

Now he was tired, his eyes feeling like someone had poured sand into them and his crotch feeling like it was crawling with unwelcome small livestock.

He needed a bath and a proper shave and about forty-eight hours of uninterrupted sleep, both of which would probably have to wait until he got back to Denver.

Longarm stepped down onto the platform at Atlanta and walked over to the line of carts to wait for his bags to be brought forward from the baggage car. He saw the Gladstone first and lifted it down from the cart, then quickly found his battered old carpetbag and picked it up, too.

When he turned around he found himself practically nose to nose with a large man wearing a scruffy blue coat. The fellow was nearly as wide as he was tall and looked like there was not an ounce of fat on him. A smaller version of himself, brass button coat and all, was standing close behind him. Both wore pressed felt helmets identifying them as police. Both also wore grimly menacing expressions.

"You all gonna haf t' come with me," the larger and nearer of them said with a scowl.

"You don't understand, boys," Longarm began.

The local cop cut him off, reached behind his back, and produced a stout billy club.

"Don' give me no back talk, boy, or I bust yo' head wide open. You unnerstan' me, boy? Well, you damn well bet-tuh. Now you come quiet or you come hard, but you gonna come with me raht damn now."

With that the cop raised his billy ready to strike.

The fellow's timing was not good. Longarm was simply in no mood for such shit.

Normally he would laugh and show his badge and offer to buy the local boys a beer.

Today he was cranky and weary and in no mood to be shaken down by a pair of local clowns.

Longarm opened his fists and let his bags drop. Before they hit the platform boards the knuckles of his right hand drove into the policeman's throat while his left blocked any attempt by the man to strike out with the billy.

The cop gagged and doubled over, grasping his throat and desperately trying to suck in some air.

His pal stood immobile, obviously shocked by this stranger's response to the bullying tactic.

Longarm shoved the big cop aside, took a step forward, and launched a powerful underhand right into the second cop's unprotected solar plexus. Every vestige of the smaller cop's breath was driven out of his lungs and he too doubled over, gasping for breath and alternately trying to puke his guts out.

Judging from the contents of the fellow's stomach, now on public display on the grimy boards of the railway platform, he had had a very large breakfast not too very long before.

By then the first was beginning to recover. His face was scarlet with a combination of fury and shame. People up and down the platform were staring in wide-eyed amazement.

But then they very likely were accustomed to the shakedown tactics of the local law but decidedly not used to seeing anyone successfully resist.

The cop straightened up, tottered for just a moment until he regained his balance, then once again lifted the billy club.

"Old son, d'you try t' hit me with that stick of yours, I promise you two things. The first is that I will for damn sure bust the arm that you're holdin' it with. The second that I will shove it up your hairy ass."

The cop looked uncertain about his next move. He glanced behind him and saw that his partner was still in distress, on his knees now and still trying to get some air back into his lungs.

His next move was to reach for the whistle that hung on a cord around his neck.

"Blow that whistle, bub, and it will be goin' down your throat before your friends have time t' come rescue you," Longarm snarled.

The cop blinked and looked undecided about his next move.

"Now," Longarm said, "if you will listen for 'bout half a moment, I'm a deputy United States marshal travelin' on official business. So back the fuck off."

"I, uh, I . . ." The cop took half a step backward, the hand holding the billy falling to waist level.

Longarm pulled his wallet out and flipped it open to display his badge. "Now get outta my way," he said.

He bent, retrieved his carpetbag and the Gladstone, and walked away from the two red-faced and impotently furious local police officers.

Longarm did not bother to look back.

Chapter 5

Longarm hailed a hack and asked to be taken downtown. The truth was that he wanted to get the hell out of the vicinity of the railroad for the time being. After all, he could handle two not very competent policemen easily enough but suspected he might have a bit of trouble if there were a dozen of them.

"Where to, mister?"

"A hotel. Something clean and decent and not too expensive," he said.

"Mister, I don't mean to speak out of turn, but that is a pistol I see there, isn't it."

"Yes, sir."

"You might think about taking that thing off and putting it away in your bags. The police around here aren't real understanding about such things."

Longarm laughed. "Reckon I already discovered that." The laugh turned into a grin. "But they can be reasoned with."

"Really?" The hack driver shook his head. "Sure wish you could teach me that trick."

"They give you a hard time, do they?"

"They surely do. There's one big fellow in particular. He's rough on newcomers. I'm surprised he didn't give you a hard time. What he wants, of course, is to be bought off. Give him five dollars of that Yankee money and he can be right agreeable. Otherwise he's apt to bust a man's head open. He's a mean one, he is."

"What's his name?"

"Otis, it is. Constable Robert Otis."

"I've changed my mind," Longarm said, leaning forward and peering up at the driver on his high seat. "Take me to the police station, please."

Three quarters of an hour later—with a scathing official complaint sitting on the precinct commander's desk, signed and sworn to by Deputy United States Marshal Custis Long—Longarm strode outside to the waiting hack for the rest of the journey to the Piedmont Hotel.

He gave the hack driver a more-than-generous tip and turned his bags over to a bellboy wearing a suit that made him look like the youngest admiral in the history of naval warfare. The room he was assigned was on the third floor, and it was a damned good thing the bellhop was there to handle the bags because Longarm was not entirely sure he could have carried them up there himself.

As the cab driver had suggested, though, the room was clean and pleasant and there was a nice enough view of Peachtree Street.

"I'm gonna need water for a bath, son."

The bellboy smiled and said, "Right in here, sir. Hot and cold running water, all you want. This valve here is for the hot. This one is cold."

"I'll be damned. What'll they think of next?" He gave the kid a nickel and very gratefully shut the door. He was filthy and wanted that bath but was so tired he did not even want to go down for supper. Food would just have to wait until morning.

Longarm slept like a lump until just before dawn, rose and lighted the gas lamps on the wall, then returned to the bathroom—there was hot and cold water in a porcelain sink, too—and shaved while standing on a floor that did not bump or sway. He had to be extra careful around the spot where he had cut himself while on the train, but it was already beginning to heal. A few more days and it should be gone.

He dressed in clean clothing, regretting that he would not be remaining in one place long enough to have laundry done, then tugged on the bell cord—another fine luxury—to summon a bellhop for his bags.

"Hold those at the desk for me, son. I'll be having breakfast before I check out."

"Yes, sir." The kid touched the front of his flat, brimless hat in salute and quickly disappeared with the bags.

Longarm ambled downstairs, more comfortable than he had been in days, and found the dining room, where he added a huge breakfast to his hotel bill. When he was done there he went out to the lobby and signed a voucher to cover his stay, then signaled the boy to fetch his things.

Out on the sidewalk along Peachtree he was amazed. In the hotel he was isolated from Atlanta, hotels of necessity being populated by transients. Here, on the street, he was exposed to the queen city of the south.

"Lordy," he breathed to a fat black man wearing a uniform that made even the bellboys look drab in comparison. "Will you look at those women!"

The doorman chuckled, his mirth belying a mumbled, "Oh, I wouldn't know, suh. It not fo' me to say."

"Huh!" Longarm snorted. "Don't bullshit me. You're a man, same as me, an' you see what's walking past here. Lordy," he repeated.

The ladies of Atlanta, pairs of them streaming past on their way to their shopping or socials or some damn things, were without question the most gorgeous creatures he had laid eyes on, one better than the next. Tall and slender and fit, not a hair out of place nor a stitch gone awry.

Longarm figured a man could lose his heart half a dozen times an hour just by standing on a street corner in Atlanta, Georgia. He only wished he had the leisure to do exactly that.

With a sigh he said, "Reckon I'll be needin' a hackney t' carry me to the East Point station."

"Yes, suh," the doorman said. But the fellow was still chuckling under his breath when he said it.

Chapter 6

"End of the line, folks. All out for Savannah." The conductor came treading easily down the aisle, oblivious of the swaying floor, and passengers began to stand and collect their belongings from the racks overhead.

Longarm let them go ahead of him. He was in no hurry. He waited until the railway coach was clear, then made his way down onto the platform, collected his bags, and went in search of a hack to take him to the waterfront.

"I expect I need a ship's broker," he told the cab driver.

"Passenger or cargo, sir?"

"Passenger," Longarm said, heaving his bags inside the shiny carriage and climbing in after them.

The driver snapped his whip well above the ears of his sway-backed nag and the coach rolled into motion. Twenty minutes later they stopped and the driver called down, "Here y' be, sir."

Longarm got out and collected his bags, paid the driver, and carried his things to a dockside kiosk whose sign announced: BILLINGSLEA AND CORDELE, BROKERS.

An aging man sat inside the kiosk alternately reading

a newspaper and munching on a banana. The fellow looked up at Longarm's approach. "Help you, sir?"

"Ever hear of a place called Fort Marion?" Longarm asked.

The ticket agent gave him a foul look that suggested he thought Longarm was pulling his leg. "That's a damn fool question. Of course I know Fort Marion. It's at St. Augustine. Used to be a Spanish fort way back before Florida became part of the U.S."

"Can I get there from here?" Longarm asked.

"Does a dog have fleas? Hell yes, you can get there from here. I can get you almost anyplace from here. That's what I do, see."

"Fine. I need t' get to Fort Marion."

"I can ticket you on the *Willard Sink*," the man said.

"Sink?" Longarm answered. "Isn't that a pretty lousy name for a boat?"

"That it is," the agent agreed, "but it's the owner's name and he is entitled to name her anything he likes. Do you want to travel on her or don't you?"

"I do," Longarm said.

"She leaves day after tomorrow."

"Don't you have anything sooner?" Longarm asked.

The agent nodded. "Of course I do. I have a ship going to Jamaica this very afternoon. Or a coaster heading for New Jersey, New York, up that way. Would you like passage on one of those?"

"But I'm going . . ."

"Yeah, so you said," the broker put in, "and that would be the *Willard Sink* leaving day after tomorrow."

"Then I expect I'll take passage on that one, thanks." Longarm pulled out his sheaf of travel vouchers and peeled one off. The ticket agent gave him a sour look. Longarm guessed there was not as much profit in the voucher as there would have been had he paid in cash. But the man accepted the government's promise to pay without spoken protest.

"Is there a hotel . . ."

The agent was already pointing up the quay toward what looked like a large and once-elegant house that had been converted for transient lodging. "Ask for Miss Judith. She'll take care of you until time for you to board ship."

"Thanks." Longarm accepted the ticket the agent handed him, picked up his bags, and headed for the rooming house.

Miss Judith looked like she had to be on the plus side of a hundred. Longarm suspected the little old lady might have been a great beauty in her day.

She led him to a tidy and immaculately clean room with a view out over the docks. It had a wingback chair positioned beside the window, but Longarm was more interested in living life than observing it from a second-floor window. He put his bags down and went back downstairs, out the door, and down the street to a waterfront saloon.

"You got rye whiskey?" he asked the barman.

"Sure. That or anything else you're like to name," the man answered.

"A rye then. Glass, not a shot."

The bartender poured and shoved the tin mug of whiskey across the bar. "Fifty cents."

Longarm paid and took his whiskey to a tiny table in the shadows at the back of the place so he could observe the underside of life in this very unfamiliar city.

He had to admit that the saloon owner kept a most eclectic group of whores black, white, and yellow. The only thing they lacked was a red Indian. He thought perhaps he should find one of those in Denver and ship her out here so the collection would be complete.

Not that he was interested in making use of any of them. They looked like they could keep medical science busy for quite some time identifying new and wonderful diseases.

He shook his head and took a sip of his rye—it was perhaps the worst rye whiskey he had ever been served, anywhere—then tipped his chair back and reached for a cheroot.

So much for Savannah, he thought. Call him when the *Willard Sink* was ready to sail.

Chapter 7

The *Willard Sink* was a side-wheel coastal steamer, perhaps two hundred feet long and a quarter of that wide. It carried a mix of cargo and passengers, the afterdeck devoted to cargo and the foredeck to steerage passengers. Longarm had not thought to ask for a stateroom but apparently the government was paying for one—a little extra profit for the ticket broker, he supposed.

The deckhand who helped him aboard led him to a tiny cubicle on the starboard side of the ship. Longarm had seen broom closets that were larger. Still, it did offer a bunk and a bit of privacy. And he did not expect to be in it all that much anyway.

"There's a lounge topside," the sailor told him. "Smoking in the after lounge only. You'll see where. Meals are in the salon. Is there anything else you need, sir?"

"This is fine, thanks." Longarm stowed his bags under the bunk and lay down to try it out. As he half expected, it was too short for his long, lean frame. He would have to sleep bent in half. Even so it was far better than the steerage passengers had. They had to sleep in the open weather wherever they could find a place to lie down—if indeed they could find a place to lie—and they were not permitted entry to the lounge or the salon.

Longarm took a look around the boat, familiarizing himself with the facilities, then settled onto a chaise in the lounge with a cigar and a scotch whiskey, there not being any rye aboard.

"Hello."

He opened his eyes and looked up. He smiled. "Are all the women in Georgia this beautiful?" he asked.

"I wouldn't know," the lady standing above him said. "Personally, I'm from Virginia."

"Once upon a time, I was from West by God Virginia and I surely do not remember the ladies there looking like you do."

This woman had light brown hair, startlingly green eyes, and a figure to make a man lose all common sense. He guessed her age around thirty, give or take a little.

"Why, thank you, sir. May I ask you something?" She helped herself to a seat on the chaise beside his.

"O' course."

"Do you always wear a gun?"

He nodded. "Ayuh, I do."

"Why?"

"In case I need t' shoot somebody o' course."

She laughed.

"Actually I'm bein' serious about that," he said. "A gun don't do you no good at all if it's back in your room inside a suitcase or some damn thing. Only place it's going t' do what it's made for is t' have it in your hand or awful close to that."

"Have you ever shot anyone?" she asked.

"Yes."

"Would you tell me about it?"

"No."

She feigned a shudder and licked her very full, red lips. She was one of those women who are excited not by knowing danger themselves but in being with dangerous men. It was something he had seen before. Did not pretend to understand, but he had certainly come across her sort many a time before now.

"Will you let me touch it?"

"No."

"Please?"

"No." He looked away.

The lady—if she was a lady, which he doubted— reached out and touched his arm. He looked at her and lifted an eyebrow. Her breathing was becoming rapid and a flush crept into her cheeks.

"Have you killed anyone? Except in the war, I mean."

Longarm nodded slowly. Very deliberately dropped his gaze to her bosom and kept his eyes there, which she could quite certainly see. "D'you want to fuck?" he asked.

The woman gasped. One hand flew to her throat while the other clenched into a tight fist.

She said nothing so again he looked away as if he had no interest in further conversation.

"Yes," she whispered, her voice hoarse and low. "Yes, please."

Longarm stubbed out the cigar he had been smoking, set his whiskey tumbler down on the side table, and stood. "Come along then," he said and strode away without looking back.

He could hear the woman scurrying to catch up behind him.

Chapter 8

"Let me . . . oh, this is so exciting," she babbled. "Let me do this, please. I've always wanted . . . please."

The woman squeezed past him and checked the lock on the stateroom door, then began quickly shedding her clothing. It turned out that she was not wearing terribly much beneath her prim and proper traveling dress. What she had been wearing very soon lay tumbled on the narrow bunk.

Longarm knew from his previous trial that there was not room on that bed for him alone, much less so for the two of them. And the floor would seem to be out of question. Probably the best thing, he thought, would be to bend her over the bed and take her from behind. There was certainly nothing wrong with that approach.

He came near to being shocked when she untied her chemise and removed it, however.

The woman's tits were bruised. Hell, they went past bruised. Rather than being merely black and blue they were purple and dark, deep red. Her flesh had been very seriously abused there, and there were bruises as well on the insides of her thighs.

She did have a good body though. Narrow waist, sturdy legs. And a huge swell of tit.

They say that anything more than a mouthful is wasted, but there was nothing wasteful about those magnificent boobs. If they had not been so battered and colorful, they would have been beautiful.

"Has someone been hurting you?" he asked.

She smiled. "Yes, and I loved it. It was wonderful, really. I hope you will hurt me, too."

"I, uh . . ."

She stepped forward, took his hands, and placed them on her tits. "Squeeze them. Please."

He did but gently.

"No, hard. Please. Really, really hard."

"I, um, I don't know as I can do that," he said.

"Oh, I do love to be hurt there. Please do it."

Longarm shook his head. "No, I don't think so."

The woman looked disappointed, but she pressed herself against him, lifting her face to his and kissing him. Her tongue probed Longarm's mouth. She tasted of cinnamon and cloves. She ground her pelvis hard against him.

When he began to disrobe, she stopped him. "Let me do it for you. Let me do everything for you."

"All right."

She pushed his coat off his shoulders and tossed it onto the bed atop her things, then unbuckled his gun belt and dropped that on top of the clothing.

When she saw the bulge that had come up at his crotch she smiled and squealed with pleasure. She deftly unbuttoned his fly, reached inside, and pulled his cock out where it stood at throbbing attention.

"Oh, my. It's huge. Are you sure you won't hurt me, please?"

"I'm sure," he mumbled, lightly touching her left tit and leaning down to get a finger in her cunt.

"Oh," she squealed again. Loudly this time.

Longarm heard a metallic click behind him and turned to see the stateroom door swing open.

A squat man wearing a brown suit and yellow spats stepped inside. The man had a tiny, break-top revolver in his hand. An Iver Johnson .32, Longarm guessed. Not all that bad a gun if you wanted something small and nasty.

He glanced toward his own .45 lying in a tangle of leather and cloth on the bed.

"Help me, Donnie," the woman cried. "He forced . . . see what he's done to me." She fluttered her hands to indicate her own purpled tits and began to cry.

The ability to break into tears without provocation must be handy in her line of work, Longarm thought.

"Rapist," the newcomer accused. "Fiend." He scowled and waved the .32 in Longarm's direction. "Hold still while I call the ship's captain. He can put you in chains until we reach Brunswick."

"Oh, surely," Longarm drawled, "there must be some way we can avoid bringing the law into this."

"No. Never," the man swore. "You have dishonored my wife, sir, and you must pay."

"Donnie, can't we think of some way we can all be satisfied," the "wife" put in.

"Well . . . perhaps," Donnie conceded.

"Well hell," Longarm said, "we all three know this is but the old badger game. So how much d' you two want from me?"

Donnie smirked. He was not a particularly handsome

man, his face florid and his mustache straggly and
unkempt. The woman, whatever the hell her name was and
whatever their relationship, probably outweighed him by
twenty pounds.

"We might . . . for a consideration," he began.

"How much of a consideration?" Longarm asked.

"Well . . ."

"Let me see what I have here," Longarm suggested.
Smiling, he dipped into his vest pocket.

And came up with his .41 derringer. "Ah. See what 'tis
that I have." He cocked the little pistol and said, "Mine's
bigger'n yours, Donnie. What's more, in my wallet layin'
in the pocket of my coat yonder is a badge 'cause what I
am is a deputy U.S. marshal and . . ."

Before Longarm could finish his sentence Donnie and
the woman—he had been right, she was no lady—had
scampered the hell out of his stateroom and disappeared
down to the main deck. She grabbed her dress in passing
but left her chemise and her shoes before running naked
into the passageway. Likely the two caused quite a stir
among the other passengers.

Longarm had no idea where the two went, but he never
got a glimpse of either one of them the entire trip down
the coast. He was more than a little pissed off, though, that
the damn woman left him with a hard-on and no place to
put it.

He had been more than ready to have a piece of that,
only to be left with the inclination but not the wherewithal.

Chapter 9

St. Augustine proved to be small. And old. Longarm was accustomed to the West where any town more than ten years old was considered practically ancient, but St. Augustine had the same aged feel as Santa Fe. Narrow streets, old buildings, and semitropical plants.

The town and the waterfront were dominated by the huge, gray presence of Fort Marion, tall and square and intimidating with its cannon pointed out to sea. Originally a Spanish fort, now the Stars and Stripes flew over its ramparts.

It was late afternoon when the *Willard Sink* arrived at the quay. Longarm allowed a skinny black kid to wrestle his bags away from him and carry them to a waterfront hotel half a block from the old fort.

"Will you be staying with us long?" asked the old woman behind the counter.

"I dunno," Longarm told her. He laid a voucher in front of her. "Official visit, y'see. I'll finish fillin' this out when I check out."

The old lady nodded and tucked the voucher away in a

drawer without questioning it. But then being so close to
the fort she probably was accustomed to seeing government paper.

"We don't serve meals," she said, "but there is a good
restaurant two doors down. If you like they can run a tab
for you and bill it through us. When you leave I will add
that to your voucher so you won't need any cash for your
meals."

"That sounds mighty accommodating," Longarm told
her. "Convenient."

"We try to be." She opened another drawer, rummaged
through it for a moment, and produced a key. "Room
three," she said. "Upstairs to your left. It has a nice view of
the bay." She smiled. "I hope you enjoy your stay with us."

"Thank you, ma'am."

Longarm mounted the staircase, the black kid following with his bags. Room three was small and clean and
smelled slightly musty. He gave the boy a dime and set his
bags inside the large mahogany wardrobe that dominated
the room, then opened the window.

The old lady was right. The view across the dancing
blue water went past being merely nice. It was magnificent.

He sat by the window and smoked a cigar, then went
down to investigate that restaurant she mentioned. Anton
Gardner could sit in his cell another night before they had
to start the long journey back to Denver and a trial before
a federal magistrate.

An hour later, his belly warm and full, Custis Long
returned to his room in the long, tropical twilight.

The door was standing slightly ajar, definitely not the
way he had left it, and there was a light burning inside the
room. He had not left that, either.

He did not carry much of great value in his bags, but

everything there was, by damn, his and he did not want some sneak thief pawing through his things.

Longarm decided to give the son of a bitch rope to hang himself with. So to speak. He wanted to give the bastard time enough to finish with his thieving, then take him down with the evidence on him.

He flattened himself against the wall next to the door leading into his room.

And waited.

Chapter 10

The door was pulled open and Longarm tensed. As soon as he saw a sleeve cuff move into his line of sight he gave a shout and launched himself at the son of a bitch. Hit chest high and drove the bastard backward, both Longarm and the intruder winding up on the floor with Longarm on top.

"Help! Rape!"

"What?"

"You . . . aren't trying to rape me?"

"Jesus! I . . . I'm sorry."

Longarm rolled off the young woman and, embarrassed, helped her onto her feet.

"I'm sorry," he repeated. "I thought . . ."

She laughed. "You thought I was robbing you. Actually I was lighting your lamp and turning down your bed."

"You work here," he said, taking time now to get a good look at the young woman. She was lovely. Slender and small and dark. Part black, he thought, with maybe some Spanish thrown in somewhere along the way. Big eyes and high cheekbones. Hair like black silk, worn long and straight. Full lips. Very, very pretty. "Did I hurt you?" he asked.

"Not . . . I'm all right." But she was holding herself stiff.

"Did you hurt your back?"

"It, um, wasn't my back. Exactly." She laughed and added, "I came down pretty hard on my backside." When she laughed she showed her teeth, very white against mocha-colored flesh. She reached behind her and rubbed her butt.

Longarm took her by the elbow and guided her to the bed. "Sit down. What can I get you? What can I do for you?"

"Nothing. I'm fine. Really."

"What's your name, miss?"

"Licia." She smiled. She was even prettier when she smiled, he noticed. "And you are Mr. Long. I saw your name on the guest register. You're a government man. I saw that, too."

"I'm Custis, not 'mister' anything. Are you sure I didn't hurt you?"

"Not very much anyway," she said, rubbing her butt again.

"Look, I really want to do something to make up for leaping on you like that. I've already had dinner tonight, but tomorrow. Could I take you to dinner tomorrow evening?"

She looked shocked. "Me. Go out with a white gentleman? Oh, Mr. Long . . . Custis, I mean . . . there's Ku Kluxers hereabout. They would get after me for sure if I was to do something like that. They might even try to do something mean to you."

He thought for a moment, then it was his turn to smile. "Do you like picnics?"

"Oh, I've never been on a picnic."

"Then tomorrow, how about you and me go on a picnic. Where would you like to go?"

"There's the island," she suggested.

Longarm raised an eyebrow. "Island?"

"Just across the inlet. Over there." She pointed toward the window. "It's the land you can see out there, across from the docks. Nobody lives over there. It's quiet and it's nice. Can you row a boat?"

"Of course I can row a boat." He smiled. "Not that I've had much practice, you understand. But I can do it sure enough."

"I have a friend who has a boat."

"You'll go then?" he asked.

Licia nodded. "A picnic would be fun, I think. If anybody sees us they will think I'm going as your servant girl. Nobody has to know the difference. Unless"—she suddenly seemed shy—"unless it is a servant that you want on your picnic."

Longarm shook his head. "I don't want no servants. I want t' have a picnic with a pretty girl, that's all. Will you come with me?"

Licia laughed and nodded. "I'd like to, Mr. . . . I mean, Custis." Her dark eyes sparkled. "A picnic. Me. Who would have thought. Oh, yes, I'd like to go on a picnic with you, Custis."

"All right then, that's settled. A picnic. Tomorrow noon?"

"Yes. Oh, yes."

"I'll have the restaurant over there pack a basket. You can meet me on the quay about noon."

"Yes, but you must remember to let me carry the basket." She laughed again. "I'm your servant girl, remember."

"I'll try an' keep that in mind." He helped her to her feet and walked to the door with her. "Are you sure you're all right? I didn't hurt you?"

"I'm fine," Licia said.

Longarm felt an impulse to kiss the girl and almost did so before he realized and put a damper on it.

After she was gone he wondered what Licia would have done had he indeed leaned down to kiss her.

Chapter 11

"You'll be wanting to see Major Ballard," the sentry told him. "He's the adjutant, sir. First door on your left after you enter the fort." The soldier returned Longarm's credentials and stood at attention until Longarm turned away, then resumed a parade rest position.

Longarm crossed the wooden bridge leading to the fort's entrance. He guessed the bridge might once have been a drawbridge, but now it was permanently in place with no chains to pull it up. Besides the moat, such as it was, was empty now except for some trash that had accumulated over time. It might once have held water but did so no longer.

There was an L-shaped corridor to gain the actual fort, obviously designed to make a land attack more difficult, and an actual iron portcullis secured above the entrance. It was an item Longarm had heard of but never seen before outside drawings in books.

But then this was, after all, an ancient Spanish fortress and he supposed he should have expected that form of architecture. The thing that truly amazed him was the material this fort was built with.

From a distance it looked like ordinary gray granite. Up close it was something very different. From close up he could see that what he thought was rock was actually composed of countless tiny seashells embedded in . . . something, he had no idea what.

"Excuse me. Soldier?"

"Yes, sir?"

"This, um, stuff. It isn't stone. So what the hell is it?"

The young soldier smiled. "Most visitors wonder about that, sir. It's called coquina. From those little shells. They're mostly coquina shells. Coquina rock can be sawed to shape fairly easily. A lot easier than rock. And it's kind of elastic. They tell me if a solid cannon ball hits, it absorbs the ball and bounces it off without shattering. Excellent stuff to build a fort from." He smiled. "Of course nowadays anyone attacking would just use an exploding shell, but I suppose those weren't available back in the old days."

"No, I suppose not. Thank you."

"Yes, sir." The young man gave Longarm an entirely unnecessary salute and went on about his business while Longarm paused at the first door to the left of the portcullis.

An enlisted man with corporal's stripes on his sleeves was seated behind a cluttered desk.

"Excuse me."

"Yes, sir. What can I do for you?"

"I'm the deputy marshal here t' pick up Anton Gardner."

"Oh, yes." The clerk made a sour face. "We'll be glad to be shut of him, marshal. I suppose it's Major Ballard you'll be wanting to see. Let me tell him you're here." The corporal stood and disappeared into a back room. He returned a moment later. "The major will see you now, sir."

Longarm removed his Stetson and stepped through the doorway.

Ballard was a small man with a large mustache. He had the crossed cannon of an artilleryman on his collar tabs and the gold oak leaves of a major on his epaulettes. He stood to greet Longarm and extended his hand to shake.

"Brightman tells me you're the man they sent to pick up Gardner."

"Yes, sir, I am."

"Good. It's a nuisance having to keep him under guard. It's bad enough having all those damned Indians. Gardner being a white civilian we've had to keep him separate." Ballard grunted. "Damned nuisance."

"Indians?" Longarm asked.

"First it was Seminoles. Now it's Apaches. I don't know what the War Department is thinking, saddling us with all those redskins. We are a military installation, not a damned prison. But please, excuse me for ranting. It is one of my pet peeves. Anyway, back to your man Gardner. I will be very happy to turn him over to you, but first may I have your extradition papers?"

"Of course, Major." Longarm reached inside his coat, extracted the signed forms Henry had given him back in Denver, and handed them over to Ballard.

"I'll have my clerk make out all the authorizations. Can you come back this afternoon and we will complete the transfer?"

"Major, I haven't figured out just yet how I wanta do this. The *Willard Sink* won't be northbound again for another week. I know that much, an' I'm not sure about any other ship goin' north. Anyway it's west I need t' go. I'm thinkin' t' maybe go overland."

"If I may offer a suggestion?" Ballard said.

"Happy t' hear one since I'm plenty off my own range down here."

"You could travel due west to the Gulf coast and catch a timber ship at Cedar Key. There is a road that leads straight from here to there, marshal. It might well be quicker than going through Georgia. You could take a ship to Galveston and take the railroad from there."

"I like that, Major. Thank you." Longarm frowned in thought. "Could I secure the use of a wagon and team to make that trip? I intend t' keep Gardner in leg irons. He won't be able t' set a horse that way, but I'm thinking it's for the best."

"I don't have a wagon you could use, Marshal, but I'm sure you can find something in town."

"Reckon I'll do that this afternoon then, an' pick Gardner up first light tomorra."

"Good enough, Marshal. I'll have your copies of the paperwork ready for you. And Gardner, of course."

Longarm stifled an unexpected impulse to salute—Lordy, hadn't it been a long time since he wore a uniform and had to do such things—executed a fairly respectable about-face, and left the major's office.

Up on the sunbaked ramparts a squad of artillerymen were going through dry-fire drills with the thoroughly modern cannon emplaced there. Longarm smiled as he walked over to the restaurant to have them make up that picnic basket he promised Licia.

He smiled, wondering how her backside felt this morning.

Chapter 12

"You're even prettier than I remembered," Longarm said.

The girl's dark complexion became even darker as she blushed. She was slender and graceful and lovely in the bright sunshine. She wore a shapeless shift that hid her figure. She took the heavy picnic basket from him despite his protests.

"It must look that I am your servant girl." She smiled. "Perhaps even your plaything, yes?"

"Now it's my turn t' blush," Longarm said. "That ain't what I invited you for."

"I know that. If I did not, I would not have agreed to come today," Licia said. "Now give me the basket, and I will walk two steps behind you as a proper little nigger should."

"I don't like t' hear you talk like that," he said.

"But it is what I am so do not worry about it. Come now. The boat is over there at the end of the dock. Uncle Jimmy is waiting and he needs to get home to bed. He fishes all night and sleeps in the day."

"At night?" Longarm asked. "How can he see to fish then?"

"He takes a lantern and hangs it on a long pole. When the fish come to the light he throws the cast net. At dawn people come to buy his fish. He has done this for many, many years. And he is not really my uncle, but I have known him all my life and think of him as an uncle." She laughed, the sound of it like small bells. "Besides, that is what everyone calls a gray-haired old nigger."

"That ain't a word I'm accustomed to hearing," Longarm said.

"It must be nice to live in a place where a white man would look at a black girl as a woman and not an object."

"Some do," Longarm said. "But not so many."

"Here is Uncle Jimmy's boat, Custis."

The craft was heavily built, perhaps twenty feet long or a little more, flat bottomed and rugged. The oars had been left in it for them but Uncle Jimmy's nets and other equipment were stored on shore somewhere.

Licia seated herself in the stern, taking the fully laden picnic basket with her. Longarm sat on the much-worn center bench and took up the oars while Licia cast the lines off.

The boat was difficult to row, both because of the weight and because it was so wide, but after fifty yards of struggling Longarm got the hang of it and pulled strongly toward the shore of the low-lying island on the other side of the inlet.

He grinned. "I like this seating arrangement," he said after a bit. "Good view behind me."

"Of the fort and the city?"

"Nope," he said. "Of the girl."

"You're going to make me blush again."

"Why? You're a remarkable beauty. Surely you know that."

Licia shook her head. "There are other girls prettier. I'm just plain."

"If there's any prettier, I ain't seen them," Longarm assured her.

They reached the island and Longarm beached the boat. Licia jumped out, took the painter, and tied them off to a gnarled palmetto root. She reached for the picnic basket but Longarm told her, "Not now that we ain't being seen. It's the gentleman supposed t' do the heavy lifting."

Licia said nothing but she looked pleased. "This way, I think. We can walk across this spit of land. There's a beach on the other side and we can probably find driftwood if you want to build a fire."

"I do. I brought a flask o' coffee and a pot to heat it in. Got pierogies with lobster meat in 'em, fried chicken, fried fish if you'd rather that sort o' thing, butter rolls, and cornbread. And some blackberry tarts for dessert. How does all that sound?"

Licia clapped her hands with delight. "I think I'm going to like picnics."

"Seein' a smile like that one makes me wish I could take you on a picnic every day," Longarm said. "Come on now. Show me where you'd like t' have this picnic. An' then later we can take a swim if you like."

"Oh, I didn't bring clothes for bathing."

He grinned. "Neither did I."

"I think I'm going to blush again," Licia said.

Chapter 13

Licia lifted her face toward the sky and closed her eyes. "I love it out here," she said. "The air is so clean and clear. No smoke like in town. No people. Eden must have been like this."

"I'm glad you're enjoyin' it," Longarm said. "Another pierogi?" He extended the folded napkin holding the remaining two lobster pierogies to her.

The girl smiled. "Thank you, no. I couldn't hold another bite."

"D'you feel like swimming?" Longarm asked.

"You just want to see me naked," she accused, laughing.

He grinned. "That, too."

"All right, yes. I would love to go in the water but only to wade. I don't know how to swim."

"I won't let anything bad happen to you," he promised.

Licia stood and reached for the hem of her shift, pulling it up and over her head. She wore nothing beneath the plain garment.

"Damn," Longarm whispered. "You're even more beautiful without clothes."

Licia had skin the color of café au lait, small breasts that were high and firm, and an impossibly small waist above a most comely swell of hip. The sleek, pale flesh was set off in startling contrast by the dark mahogany hue of her nipples and the shiny black of her tightly curled pubic hair.

She stood for a moment, posing before him, obviously enjoying Longarm's appreciation of her body. Then she dropped her shift onto the sand beside their picnic blanket and, laughing, ran to the water's edge.

Longarm quickly stripped, adding his clothes to hers, and joined her. He took Licia's hand and they walked together into the water. He winced when the cold water of the Atlantic Ocean reached his cods, and Licia laughed at him. She bent, dipped up a handful of the salty water, and threw it on his chest.

Longarm took the girl into his arms and paused, looking into her clear, brown eyes. Then he kissed her. Licia closed her eyes and molded her body to his. He bent, scooped her up to cradle her against his chest, and waded deeper into the water without breaking the kiss.

Licia's tongue probed shyly into his mouth and she made a small sound deep in her throat. A sound, he thought, of contentment.

"This is lovely," she said when the kiss was broken. "The water, the sun . . . the company. I couldn't ask for a better day than this. Thank you for bringing me."

"Shh," Longarm said and kissed her again.

"Mr. Long . . . Custis . . . could we go back to the shore now? I want to feel you inside me."

Without speaking he turned and, still carrying her, walked out of the water and back to the blanket. He bent and placed Licia on her back, then lay down beside her.

Her flesh was goose-bumped from the cold water, and when he dipped his head to her nipple she tasted of the salt of the sea.

"I like that," she said as he sucked on her nipple and licked her breast.

Longarm moved on top of her. Wedged himself between her knees and reached down to guide himself inside the girl's moist, slippery pussy.

Licia's eyes went wide as she felt the size of him stretch her body to the limit.

"Are you all ri—"

"No, don't stop. It feels wonderful. So big but . . . wonderful."

Longarm stroked slowly in and out, giving her body time to adjust to his size, then gradually increased the tempo of his strokes until Licia cried out and fiercely clutched him, her arms tight around him as she reached a sudden climax.

He pounded her belly with his for another few moments until his sap came rushing out into her. Then he collapsed atop her, giving Licia his weight while they both caught their breath.

After a minute or two Longarm rolled away from her and Licia pouted, "You took it away."

Longarm grinned. "You can have it back any time y' want."

"Promise?" she asked.

He nodded. "Yeah. I promise." He kissed her and the girl sighed with contentment.

"Do you know what I would like?" she asked after a few minutes of silently watching the clouds drift overhead and listening to the sound of the waves rolled onto the white sand.

"Mm?" he mumbled.

"I would like for us to go back into the water for a few minutes to sort of, well, wash things off. Then I would like to taste you."

Longarm smiled. "I do think that's somethin' we can manage, ma'am."

Licia jumped to her feet and reached down for his hand, practically pulling him upright and leading him back to the ocean.

Picnics, Longarm thought, are a damn fine idea.

Chapter 14

The next morning Longarm was at the Fort Marion portcullis as dawn was breaking, the sun just rising out of the sea, the colors of the sunrise spectacular on a bank of low-hanging cloud. The sentry snapped to attention and offered an entirely unnecessary salute.

"Good morning, sir. The major is expecting you. He is in his office, sir. I believe you know the way."

"Thank you, Private." Longarm entered the fort, his footsteps hollow on the bridge planks, and turned to his left to Major Ballard's office. The same corporal was seated at the desk inside the doorway.

"Good morning, Marshal. I'll tell him you're here." The man disappeared into Ballard's office and was back moments later. "This way, sir."

The little artilleryman rose to greet Longarm. "I have everything ready for you. Just sign these releases, please." In a much louder voice he called, "Brightman. Bring the prisoner."

Longarm accepted a pen and vial of ink and signed for receipt of the prisoner, whom he had not yet laid eyes on

much less taken possession of. Almost as soon as he had
finished that, the corporal returned with a large and excep-
tionally hairy man wearing black-and-white-striped canvas
clothing.

Anton Gardner had wildly tangled jet-black hair, a huge
growth of black beard, and the look of a madman in his
eyes. He saw Longarm and scowled.

"Just one of you bastards? Good. I'll rip your fucking
heart out and roast it for my supper."

"Sit down, asshole," Longarm snarled back at him.
"Mind your manners like a good little boy."

"I'll 'little boy' you, you son of a bitch. Soon as we're
alone and you don't have all these bluebelly soldier boys
to protect you. And I'll sit when I damn well feel like it."

Longarm shrugged. "Fine. You feel like it now." At the
word "now" he punched Gardner in the face—hard—
pulping the man's lips and making bright blood drool down
into his beard.

Gardner sat.

Longarm brought out the heavy leg irons, the chain
linking them just long enough to allow the wearer to shuf-
fle. He fitted them around Gardner's ankles.

"We can get something straight here. Mind your manners and we can get along just fine. Show your ass like that
again and by the time we reach Denver you'll be even
uglier than you are now, you not bein' used to these here
irons and fallin' down s' often." He gave Gardner a grim
smile. "If y' know what I mean."

Gardner grunted a response that might have meant anything.

"Just so's we understand each other," Longarm said. He
turned to Corporal Brightman. "Reckon I need the key t'
your manacles. I brought my own."

They made the switch, Longarm returning the army's cuffs and replacing them on Gardner's wrists with his own.

"I want a chew," Gardner said.

"Yeah, an' I woke up this morning wantin' a piece o' ass. Reckon we're both gonna be disappointed, aren't we," Longarm responded.

"I'm hungry," the prisoner complained.

"The law says you're entitled to two meals a day," Longarm told him. "Less if you give me any shit." He turned to Ballard and thanked him, then took Gardner by the elbow and started him on his way.

They had a long way to go and Longarm already could barely stand the sight of Anton Gardner.

Chapter 15

"You expect me to ride in that broke-down piece of shit?" Gardner complained when he saw the buggy Longarm expected him to ride in.

"Truth is, Gardner, I don't care if you ride in it or not," Longarm informed the prisoner. "But I got t' tell you, it's either you crawl up in there an' ride . . . or I'll just hitch you on behind an' let the horse drag you all the fuckin' way across this here state to Cedar Key."

In truth the buggy really did look like it was ready to collapse into a heap of sticks and metal bits at the first good bump. There might once have been a top on it but that had long since disappeared. So had any paint that used to cover its nakedness. The wheels were spindly, no one matching any other in size, shape or color. The harness was old and much patched, as was what passed for upholstery on the narrow seat. And the horse pulling this contraption looked like it had seen better days, too.

Still, it was the best Longarm had been able to manage anywhere in St. Augustine, and at that he had had to purchase the outfit. No one had been willing to rent him a rig since there was no way to guarantee its return from the other side of the state.

His hope was that he could arrange to sell it once they got to Cedar Key. That would at least recoup some of the government's money.

"Climb in," Longarm ordered.

"I can't lift my leg enough to reach the step," Gardner said.

Longarm shrugged. "No problem." He reached into the box on the back of the buggy and lifted out a chain, attached one end to the buggy frame below the box and approached Gardner with the other end of the stout chain. "Hold out your hands."

"What the fuck are you doing?" Gardner demanded.

"Just what I told you. I'm gonna hook you up behind an' drag your sorry ass t' Cedar Key."

"You can't do that. It ain't humane."

"I suggest you file a complaint 'bout that when we get to Denver." Longarm chuckled. "They got forms for that an' everything."

"Put your damn chain away. Maybe I can get in the son of a bitch after all."

"Yeah. Maybe you can."

Gardner managed although he had to bend forward until he was lying on the floor half in and half out, then squirm up fully onto the floor before getting onto his knees and from there onto the seat.

"You bastard," he snarled at Longarm.

Calmly, Longarm said, "Give me any shit, mister, an' I'll chain your hands behind your back, which is within my rights, you bein' such a dangerous prisoner and all."

"I'll show you dangerous, you son of a bitch," Gardner shot back at him. "First chance I get, you're a dead man.

I'm gonna roast your heart for my own self and fry up your liver for my boys. With onions."

"Yeah, sure you are. Until then, jus' shut your ugly mouth." Longarm dropped the chain back into the old crate that was bolted onto the back of the buggy. The box already held his bags. Anton Gardner had no other clothing to worry about.

He rummaged into the Gladstone for an extra pair of handcuffs and used them to secure Gardner's right wrist to the frame of the seat. That gave the prisoner very little room to move. Too little, Longarm was hoping, for the man to cause any mayhem.

Longarm climbed onto the seat beside Gardner and unwrapped the driving lines from around the empty whip socket. He took up a light contact with the brown horse's mouth and gave the lines a shake. "H'yup, boy."

The bony animal leaned into the traces and set off at a slow walk.

Chapter 16

They had not gotten five miles out of town before Longarm discovered he had made a mistake when he bought this outfit. The buggy was light enough, but its narrow wheels cut too deeply into the loose sand that passed for soil here. That made the pull too difficult for the one aging horse. A two-up would have been much more efficient and could have made much better time on the road.

Such a change would have done nothing, though, about the dust that rose off the sand that was disturbed by the passage of horse and wheel. The fine grit, almost the consistency of a woman's face powder, quickly covered every surface on or around the buggy. It drifted inside Longarm's collar and combined with his sweat to form a black paste that chafed and annoyed.

Worse, once they got away from the coast, away from the salt-tinged sea breeze, the heat lay on them like a blanket, stifling and dreary.

Longarm removed his coat and draped it over the back of the seat. He removed his collar and, rather than crease the brittle celluloid, laid it on the floor beneath the seat.

He opened the top button of his shirt and rolled his sleeves up. Still he was so hot he found it difficult to breathe.

Every little bit he would lift his hat to let some air reach his scalp and repeatedly he wiped his face of the sweat that ran down his neck and plastered the cloth of his shirt to his ribs.

"You picked a helluva place t' run to," he snarled at Gardner. "Why couldn't you've got your ass caught up in Montana or some such?"

Gardner gave him a dirty look but said nothing.

They came to a small creek half hidden in the dense, junglelike growth and moss-hung trees that flanked the narrow road. Longarm pulled the brown to a halt and wrapped the driving lines around the empty whip socket.

Gardner edged as far away from Longarm as he could get on the seat and gave him a nervous look. "Are you gonna shoot me now, you asshole? You want me to beg? Well, fuck you. Anton Gardner don't beg from no man, not about nothing."

"What I am gonna do, shit-for-brains, is get us some water t' cool down with. Us an' the horse, too." He sighed and wiped his face again. "It's a son of a bitch down here. Damn if I can figure out why anybody in his right fucking mind would want t' live here. Not away from the ocean anyhow."

Gardner snorted. "It 'pears to me that we ain't exactly seen anybody what does live away from the ocean. Haven't seen a fucking soul since we left that town. As for what I was doing when I got caught, I was on my way to Cuba. I have me some business there." He snorted. "Still do. Which I will tend to just as soon as I gut your lawdog ass and get out of these chains."

"Boast all you like," Longarm told him, "but those chains stay in place."

Longarm had nothing to carry water in so he used his hat, watering first the horse, then himself and finally Gardner. The water was tepid, slightly bitter from tannin steeped from fallen leaves, but at least it cut through the dust.

When each of them had had enough to drink, Longarm dipped his kerchief into the creek and sponged his face and neck and arms. Better to be wet with that, he thought, than dripping with his own sweat.

"All right," he said after the restful break. "We aren't gonna get there by settin' in the middle of this road." He frowned. "If a shitty track like this can be called a road."

He climbed back into the buggy beside Gardner and once again took up the driving lines.

"If you want me to spell you driving, asshole, just unfasten me from this seat and pass me the reins."

"That'll be the fucking day," Longarm snorted.

The buggy lurched forward, grinding through the deep sand and occasionally bumping over a root.

The trip, Longarm thought, promised to be a miserable one, hot and boring.

He was wrong.

Chapter 17

They drove through what passed for a settlement. Four houses, each surrounded by weeds and sand and skittering chickens, and one store supplying the needs of families for miles around.

"Take me over to that outhouse, lawman. I got to take a shit," Gardner demanded.

"You stay chained," Longarm said.

"But I got . . ."

"Shit in your pants if you can't hold it. You ain't getting loose till we stop for the night, an' then I'll be keepin' you under a gun."

Longarm brought the buggy to a halt though and left it to go into the store. He bought bacon, rice, tinned peaches, and a handful of coffee along with a large tin can that would serve to boil the coffee in. He expected to be on the road no more than three nights and made his purchases accordingly.

When he attempted to pay with a voucher the proprietor refused to accept the promise to pay.

"Look, all you got t' do is take this to the nearest post office. They'll give you cash for the voucher."

"Shit, mister, I *am* the post office here and I never heard of no such of a thing," the rather scruffy fellow returned.

"All right then, take it to the post office in St. Augustine. You go there sometimes, don't you? Or to the fort. Major Ballard will see that you're paid."

The storekeeper folded his arms and scowled. "Mister, I ain't taking it and that's that. Now either pay cash or leave my stuff right where it sets."

Longarm paid cash. He tucked his purchases into the tail box along with his luggage and the spare trace chain he had threatened Gardner with earlier, then returned to the seat and took up the lines.

"We'll stop toward sundown," he said and set the brown horse to pulling.

Two miles later they came across a traveler in trouble. A rather attractive traveler at that.

He could not see what sort of figure she was hiding under a duster and a broad-brimmed hat but she had the face of an angel, delicate features, a tiny chin and heart-shaped mouth. And red hair. Longarm was a pushover for a handsome woman with red hair.

She stepped into the road and flagged them down.

"Trouble, ma'am?" Longarm asked.

"Oh, yes," she gasped. "My horse bolted and ran my buggy into a palmetto root. It broke an axle and I've been walking. But I am so frightened. I hear things in the jungle. Panthers, perhaps. Or bears. And I almost stepped on an ugly snake. I . . . can you help me? Please?"

Longarm sighed. He supposed the least he could do would be to take her back to that last settlement. Maybe she could get somebody from there to come fix her outfit.

"The horse is all right?" he asked.

"Yes, but . . . I have to get to Cedar Key. It is urgent."

Longarm rubbed his chin and thought for a moment. "We, uh, we're goin' to Cedar Key our own selves. I suppose . . . if your business is important . . ."

"Oh, it is. It is very important, sir."

"If you wouldn't mind ridin' in the presence of this here murdering prisoner . . ."

"Anything, sir. If you could do anything to get me there quickly, I would do anything." She batted her eyes and repeated, "Anything."

"It will be a tight squeeze on this seat. An' you'll want t' avoid setting next t' the prisoner. But if you're willing, why, I reckon you can ride along. You got luggage, ma'am?"

"It is 'miss,' not 'ma'am.' And I do have a small bag. It is in my wrecked surrey."

"That's up ahead yonder?" Longarm asked.

The girl nodded. Longarm guessed her to be thirty, give or take a bit. And with a wonderful complexion. Huge eyes, clear and blue.

"Come ahead then, miss."

He did not at all mind sitting between the girl and Anton Gardner. The girl, he noted, smelled considerably nicer than Gardner did.

They reached the site of her wreck a half mile or so farther on. A pale gray horse was still standing in the poles of a very handsome red-and-yellow surrey, the front axle of which was broken just like the lady said.

Longarm stopped the somewhat overloaded buggy and crawled across Gardner to reach the ground so he could come around and help the lady down.

He fetched her bag, a simple container little larger than a handbag, and handed it to her. "Is there anything else, miss?"

"No." She smiled. "You are awfully kind, sir. I . . . oh!"
She was holding the bag awkwardly. It came open and
spilled its contents into the loose dirt at the side of the
road.

Longarm immediately bent to retrieve the dropped articles, which seemed mostly to consist of small bottles and
stoppered vials. "Let me . . ."

He heard as much as felt a crushing blow on the back
of his head, the sound like thumping a ripe melon.

He was not even aware of the fact that he fell facedown
in the sand.

Chapter 18

Longarm groaned. Blinked sand out of his eyes. He rolled onto his side and reached up, feeling detached from his hand, and brushed sand off his face.

The redheaded bitch must have . . .

The buggy. Where was the damned buggy? And Anton Gardner?

He sat up, his head pounding like little men with big hammers were inside his skull trying to batter their way out.

It took him several tries to get his eyes to focus. When the blurriness cleared he could see the woman's surrey and his own buggy sitting where they had been, but there was no sign of either the horses or the humans.

He tried to guess how long he might have been unconscious. Not as long as those two had hoped. There was still a little daylight left although night seemed to be not very far away.

Longarm shook his head—damn, but that was a mistake—and tried to think, tried to take stock of his situation.

He checked his pockets and found that his keys were gone, both the small key to the manacles and the much larger key that opened the leg chains.

His money was gone, of course, and his Colt revolver. The derringer was still in his watch pocket, and there were spare cartridges for that in his carpetbag. Uh, if he still had the carpetbag.

Longarm struggled to his feet. It took three tries to come upright, and when he did his vision blurred and darkened. He stood for a moment until it cleared, then made his way on shaky legs to the buggy.

Both his Gladstone and the carpetbag were still in the box on the back of the buggy. Gardner's manacles and leg irons lay in the sand at the side of the buggy.

Longarm was more than a little surprised that the son of a bitch hadn't finished him off with a bullet to the back of the head while he was lying there.

But then the two of them, Gardner and the woman, might well have assumed that he was already dead. Certainly his head felt like they had every reason to think that.

He went back to where he had been lying and retrieved his hat. It was crushed at the back where the redhead had hit him with something hard and heavy. Very likely the Stetson had saved his life for a blow to the skull like that can indeed be fatal.

He needed . . . he needed about twenty-four hours of sleep was what he needed. That and half a bottle of whiskey.

The sleep would have to wait, but he had most of a bottle of rye in his carpetbag. He retrieved it and took a long, throat-cleansing drink, then replaced the cork in the bottle and put it back into his bag.

He took his coat down from the buggy seat where it had

fallen and put it on. Got a handful of .41-caliber cartridges from his bag and dropped them into his coat pocket. Grunted in annoyance at his own forgetfulness and took all the shiny brass cartridges out of that pocket, separated out the .45s that fit a revolver he no longer had and moved them to the left-hand pocket, then returned the .41s to the right-hand pocket where they would be quickly available if he needed them.

His head was still pounding furiously, but he would just have to worry about that some other time. He did take a moment to explore it with very light fingertips. He had a goose egg high on the back of his head, but there did not seem to be any blood there. Thanks to the good beaver of his Stetson, he was sure.

Longarm looked into the redhead's surrey. There was nothing of interest there.

He looked along the road to see which way the two might have gone, but the soft sand did not take hoofprints and there had been enough traffic along the road in past days to make tracking them impossible.

He was betting, however, that Gardner would be heading for wherever it was that he had been captured. The reports about the man said nothing about recovering any of the loot he and his gang had stolen in their last haul, so Gardner must have had time to hide it before someone named Craig took him into custody.

Longarm doubted the man would abandon that much money and simply ride away from it.

But wherever it was, Gardner was headed there on horseback while Longarm was afoot. And wobbly.

Standing around feeling sorry for himself was not going to accomplish anything, though.

He settled his Stetson very gingerly atop his head, squared his shoulders, and began hiking back toward that last settlement they had passed through.

And heaven help any alligators, panthers, or black bears that got in his way.

Chapter 19

"Damnit, I already done told you, you aren't getting no credit."

"And I told you, I will sign a voucher for anything I buy. Hell, I'll even give you a fifty percent premium over the regular cost. But I got to have these things. I simply got to," Longarm told the storekeeper. "Something else, mister, I need t' know has a man an' woman . . . a redhead, that one . . . come riding through here yesterday. It's important."

The obstinate storekeeper grunted. "Expect I can tell you that much for free. I haven't seen no man and woman traveling together on horseback lately."

Longarm sighed. That news made things all the worse for him. He had no choice but to go back to Fort Marion where he might hope to reequip. That meant he would be traveling directly opposite the way Gardner and the woman were going. That put him in a lousy mood already, and this man was not making things better with his stubbornness.

It had been well past dark by the time Longarm stumbled into the settlement, and the people who lived there were closed up tight for the night. Longarm settled down on the front stoop of the store and spent an uncomfortable night there. But he did feel much better in the morning.

Now he was the storekeeper's first customer of the day. And the experience was not pleasing to either of them.

"Look, I already told you . . . ," Longarm began.

The storekeeper responded with an "I already told you" of his own.

"You saw my credentials yesterday. I can't show them to you now because the prisoner who escaped stole my wallet and all my cash, too. But I still have these voucher papers and I'll give you one of those. I need a horse and a gun. It's important."

"I'm not gonna do it," the storekeeper insisted. "I'm not taking paper. I need cash money."

"You have the post office here, you said," Longarm told him.

The storekeeper nodded. "That's right, I do. You want to send a letter? Fine. But a stamp will cost you three cents, and I'm not gonna give you credit for that neither."

"Mister, I am a representative of the United States of America, a duly sworn officer o' the law. Now one way or another I'll get back to Fort Marion an' reequip. When I do I can have the postal service withdraw your . . . whatchamacallit . . . your franchise for this post office." He had no such authority but this man would not know that. "Now are you gonna take my vouchers or not?"

Longarm crossed his arms and scowled at the man.

With not very good grace the man gave in, his expression purely hateful. "I don't have no horse or gun to sell but I s'pose I can stake you to a meal." He screwed up his face in thought—something Longarm suspected he did rather seldom—and finally said, "For fifty cents on one of them voucher papers."

A normal price for a breakfast would likely be a dime, fifteen cents at most. Longarm suspected the vulture had been pondering just how far he could push his thievery now that the customer was in such need.

The storekeeper nodded decisively and reaffirmed, "Fifty cent. Take it or leave it."

Longarm signed a voucher and exchanged it for a handful of jerky—bear meat, not bad—and three dry and crumbly biscuits. He would damn near have killed for a cup of coffee to go with the dry meal but had to settle for water instead.

"Thank you," Longarm told the storekeep, doubting that the son of a bitch recognized the sarcasm in the words. "Now how can I get back to St. Augustine? I'm in a hurry."

The storekeeper inclined his head toward the east. "It's down the road that way," he said.

"I know, but how can I get there?"

The man shrugged and turned away to fuss with straightening a few of the items on his shelves.

Longarm had little choice but to resume walking down the same sand track that passed for a road here.

He had found it much easier to travel the day before when he was riding in that buggy with Anton Gardner beside him.

Chapter 20

It was late morning when Longarm presented himself at the gate of Fort Marion. He would have been much later getting there but managed to hitch a ride on a farm wagon, the driver delivering a load of sweet corn to the public market in St. Augustine.

"I wish I could pay you, but like I told you I got mugged an' robbed," Longarm told the driver when he crawled down off the wagon box.

The driver, an elderly black man with skin dark and gleaming with the oils of good health, waved the thanks away. "I'm a Christian gentleman, Marshal. Always glad to do a good service. Just consider that it comes from the Lord and give your thanks to Him."

"That I shall, sir. Thank you."

They parted at the edge of the older part of town and Longarm walked the remaining few blocks to the fort.

Now he stood in front of Major Ballard once more, a feeling of intense embarrassment tugging at him when he admitted to his folly with the damned redhead.

"I can fix you up, deputy. I can't replace your badge, of course, but I can give you a horse and a military-issue .45."

"Saddlebags and ammunition, too, sir? And handcuffs an' leg irons t' carry in the other side o' the saddlebags. I intend t' catch up with that son of a bitch, and this time he won't be getting' away from me. I can promise you that."

A very small smile pulled at Ballard's lips. "I will assume you felt he could not escape the last time, either."

Longarm sighed. "Yes, sir. That is most surely true. Oh, and one other thing, Major. Would it be too much t' ask you to send a detail out to bring that buggy back? It's government property an' it has some government gear in it, like the manacles and such. An' of course it has my bags in it, too. I'd admire t' get my things back if I can."

The major nodded and said, "I can do that, Deputy."

"Thank you, sir. I 'preciate it."

Ballard raised his voice and called, "Brightman."

Half an hour later Longarm rode out of Fort Marion on a nag taken from an artillery caisson and put under saddle. He had an artillerist's Colt in his holster. The .45 had a seven-and-one-half-inch barrel while he preferred four inches, but beggars cannot be choosers. The difference might slow his draw a little but he had no intention of allowing things to get to the point of needing a quick draw.

If Anton Gardner gave him any shit this time around, Custis Long intend to put him down with a bullet and be done with it.

And if it came to that, well, he would do the same with that bitch of a redhead.

All he had to do now was find the bastards.

Chapter 21

"Dan Craig is away somewhere, Deputy, riding circuit with the judge for this district," the clerk of federal court told him. "We may not hear from him for another week or more."

"Do you know where it was that he found Anton Gardner?" Longarm asked. "That's all I really need t' ask him about."

The clerk, who reminded Longarm of their own Henry back in Denver even though the two looked nothing alike, this man being squat and blond, shook his head. "I don't know that he ever said, deputy."

"What about his report? You had to prepare that, didn't you?"

"Dan isn't much on paperwork. I'm sure he turned something in. He must have. But I never wrote anything up beyond the fact that Gardner was in custody. And of course the wire to your marshal informing him that we had his man. None of that detailed exactly how or where Dan secured the man."

"Damn," Longarm muttered. "Can you check your records to see just what Craig put down? If anything."

"I'll check them for you, Deputy, but I won't have time to get to your request until late, possibly not until tomorrow morning. It all depends on what my marshal needs done." The man gave Longarm an apologetic smile. "He does come first here, you understand."

"Yeah. I understand." There was no point in getting pissed off about it. That would only make the man less inclined to help, and there is nothing so balky as a government employee who gets his back up about something. "Do what you can, please. I'll check in with you every little once in a while." Longarm managed a smile of his own and added a hearty "thanks, man" before he left.

There was little he could do until he found out which direction he should take from St. Augustine. Gardner and the redhead would surely be going to wherever Gardner had had a chance to hide his loot before his capture. But where the hell would that have been, that was the question.

Longarm grumbled, but he had no choice except to wait and to hope that the clerk found the information Longarm needed.

Hunger pangs sent him back to the waterfront and the café he already knew. He filled up with a good dinner of pork chops, fried fish, greens, and lima beans. And coffee. Coffee by the gallon to make up for all he had missed since the day before.

When he finally stopped eating and slurping down the stout coffee he apologized to the proprietor and explained, "I'll have t' put the waiter's tip on this voucher 'cause I got no cash. Sorry."

It occurred to Longarm that he could not keep paying for small items with his vouchers or he would soon run

out of them. So back first to the district marshal's office—
no, the clerk had no had time yet to dig into those record
files, sorry—and then to Fort Marion where once again he
presented himself before Major Ballard.

"I have another favor t' ask of you, Major."

"What is it this time, Long?" Ballard sounded a little
annoyed.

"I'm needin' some cash money in my pockets. I'd like
you t' authorize your paymaster t' give me, say, fifty dollars. I'll make out a voucher for the payment, o' course."
It occurred to him that the next time he checked with the
marshal's clerk he should probably get another fistful of
voucher forms.

Ballard grunted unhappily but said, "All right, damnit,
but then would you *please* let us get on with our work
here." The little artillerist raised his voice and yelled,
"Brightman!"

Late afternoon found Longarm with cash in his pockets
and a fresh sheaf of voucher forms in his coat but still with
no clue as to where he should start his search for Anton
Gardner and that treacherous bitch of a redhead.

The marshal's clerk, Jimmy, rolled the top down over
his desk and locked it. He shook his head and said, "Sorry,
Deputy, but I just haven't had time to look up that report.
I'll get to it tomorrow morning. I promise."

"All right, Jimmy, thanks."

Longarm reluctantly turned away. He took the army's
horse to a nearby livery and then walked back to the same
hotel he had occupied before.

And every minute he delayed, Anton Gardner would
be getting farther away. Perhaps had his hands on the stolen money by now. Probably had his hands on the redhead
by now.

The only good thing, Longarm thought, was that the two of them likely believed that the blow to his head had killed him back there on that sandy road. They would not know that cold death was stalking them.

They would run. They could not hide.

Longarm lighted a cheroot—Gardner had not taken those, thank goodness—and thought wistfully about the bottle of rye back there in his carpetbag.

Tomorrow, he thought. Jimmy would look up Dan Craig's report tomorrow.

Chapter 22

Longarm sat by the open window, hoping for a breath of fresh air to relieve some of the moist heat, when he heard a light tapping on his door. He was expecting no trouble here but palmed the long-barreled .45 Army anyway before cat-footing silently to the door and asking, "Who's there?"

"It's me, Mr. Long," a female voice returned.

"Licia?"

"Yes. Let me in, will you? I'm supposed to be doing laundry now but I have to talk to you."

He opened the door and Licia slipped in with a backward glance to make sure she was not observed being somewhere other than where she was supposed to be at this hour.

Longarm immediately took the girl into his arms and kissed her. She returned the embrace only for a moment before she placed her palms on his chest and pushed him away. "I need to talk to you. I heard you had troubles on the road."

"You heard that right," Longarm agreed. "More'n I ever wanted t' have."

"Is there any way I can help you, Mr. Long?" She blushed. "I got a soft spot for you, you know."

He sighed. "Not unless you can tell me where that son of a bitch Gardner got himself caught by the law. Marshal Craig caught him but I don't know where, an' I'm figuring he hid his stolen loot there before they took him. Figuring that's where he'll be headed now. Maybe already been there by now, him and the woman that tricked me an' let him get away."

"I wouldn't know a thing like that, Mr. Long," Licia said.

"No, o' course you wouldn't. Neither does anybody else around here, it seems. I don't even know where this Craig fella has got off to. Riding circuit with the judge, they said, but they don't know where they might be exactly."

"That's what you need to know?" Licia asked. "Where Marshal Craig caught up with that man?"

Longarm nodded. "Sure is."

"Well, is there anything I *can* do to help out, seeing as how I don't know that?" Licia asked.

He chuckled and touched her cheek. "Just one thing I can think of. If, um, if you think you can sneak in here when you get done working. For, well, you know."

The girl blushed again. "Later maybe," she whispered. "Maybe after the hotel is all quiet and sleeping. If I can. I'm not making no promises. But . . . if I can."

Longarm nodded. "I'll leave the door unlocked." He smiled and kissed her.

Licia returned his kiss, then again pulled away and slipped out the door after pausing to make sure the corridor was empty and she would not be observed.

Chapter 23

Something, some subtle shift of light or sound or air movement, woke Longarm from deep sleep. He came instantly awake, hand on his Colt and senses alert, to see a glow of light from a distant lamp or candle in the corridor outside his room and a human form outlined against that light.

He smiled and removed his hand from the revolver.

"Here," he said softly, pulling the sheet aside to make room on the bed for Licia.

She closed the door and he heard the bolt slide closed, heard the whisper of cloth slithering to the floor as she shed her dress, felt the bed tilt and then the warmth of her slender body against his.

Licia's kiss was soft. Her tongue met his then moved down to his chest. She licked his right nipple and then the left. Moved lower, across his belly to the base of his cock, flicked lightly along his shaft until she reached the engorged, bulbous head.

She peeled back his foreskin and ran her tongue around and around the head of his cock before taking it into her mouth. Not too deeply as she began to gag when it reached her throat. Longarm stroked the back of her head, reassuring her that it was not important that she could not take him any deeper.

Licia sucked on him a while longer, then pulled away and sat on top of him, her thighs straddling Longarm's hips. She reached down to guide herself onto his erection and then lowered herself, her flesh engulfing his with the warmth of her wet and very ready pussy.

Longarm rose to meet her. He felt the length of his shaft penetrate her body and fill her hot, pulsing cavity.

He heard Licia sigh at the feel of him inside her, felt the clenching of her vaginal muscles around the base of his cock.

Together they began to stroke, slowly at first and then more quickly until finally he was pounding her with his belly, until finally he exploded into her, come spurting its heat deep inside her.

Licia gasped and cried out as she reached her own powerful climax and then collapsed onto his chest, her breath coming rapidly. "Wonderful," she whispered, her cheek soft and warm on his sweat-slicked skin.

"I hafta agree with that, darlin'," Longarm said, stroking her back and rubbing the nape of her slender neck. "I'm glad you could get away."

"I had to," she said.

"Oh, I agree. This was mighty good," he told her.

"No. I . . . I mean, yes. It was wonderful. But that isn't what I meant. There is something I have to tell you. I asked around." He heard her chuckle and felt the flutter of her belly against his. "Us niggers, we know things. We see and we hear and nobody pays us no mind. Well, I asked around. Your man Gardner was captured in Lake City."

"Why does that name sound familiar?" he mused.

"There was a battle there." She sounded pleased. "Our boys whupped those Rebels. I was too little to remember it my own self but I heard about it."

"So have I," Longarm said. "That's where Gardner was when Craig caught him?"

"Sure was."

"Does this grapevine of yours say where he was heading at the time?"

"South," she told him. "But they don't know 'xactly where he was going."

"And the woman?" Longarm asked.

He felt Licia shrug. "She wasn't with him. Maybe she's what he was going to."

"Darlin' girl, you have no idea how much of a help you've been to me." Longarm rolled her off of him, leaned down and kissed her, then sat up on the side of the bed and reached for his clothes.

"What are you doing?" Licia asked.

"I'm heading for this Lake City place. Gardner likely has already been there but if I'm lucky he'll stop t' celebrate his good fortune in gettin' away from me."

"What if he didn't stop?"

Longarm grinned. "Then I'll run his sorry ass to earth wherever he's gone to ground."

He was dressed, saddled, and on his way in a half hour or little more.

Chapter 24

The artillery horse proved to be a better mount than he had any right to expect since it was the animal the artillery battery back at Fort Marion was most willing to get rid of.

It was deaf as a post of course, probably as a result of having its eardrums pierced. A good many outfits, both cavalry and artillery, did that to insure a horse would not be frightened in the face of gunfire. It was a practice Longarm disapproved because often it only served to make the animal even more spooky since they could not hear what was coming and could be startled by everything. Still, this big brown creature seemed to suffer no such effects.

It was an older horse, wide in the barrel and with a bobbed tail. It stood close to seventeen hands and did not neck-rein, but its trot was smooth and fast and it could hold the gait seemingly without end.

Longarm took the road back to the asshole storekeeper's village at a steady pace, letting the big horse hold to the trail without much guidance from its rider. But then the horse's night vision was far better than Longarm's.

He rode through the darkened settlement without pause. But he did lift a middle finger to the storekeeper as he passed by.

He reached the abandoned buggy and surrey in the wee hours of the morning and stopped there to retrieve a few items from the luggage he had left in the buggy. He hoped he would see the carpetbag and the Gladstone again sometime, but if he did not, there was nothing in them that could not be replaced.

He transferred a box of spare cartridges and his bottle of rye to the army-issue saddlebags behind his McClellan and filled whatever space was left in them with a few extra shirts and underwear. Then he climbed back onto the brown and resumed the road-eating trot.

Daybreak found him on a road leading north, toward—he hoped—Lake City. If there had been any signposts or markers, he missed seeing them in the dark, but this was his best guess.

He did not want to make a false start and have to retrace his steps. But then when he thought about it, Gardner and the woman were already far ahead of him. He needed to think of this chase as a distance event and not a sprint.

And he intended to get to the finish line, however long it took.

"C'mon, y' old son of a bitch," he muttered to the brown.

The deaf horse did not so much as twitch an ear at the sound of his voice.

Chapter 25

If the settlement had a name he did not know what it was. For that matter really did not care. It was daylight. There was a store. And his belly was shaking hands with his backbone.

Longarm dismounted, his butt and knees damned grateful for the respite, and tied the brown horse to the trunk of a tree with leaves so shiny they looked like they had been waxed. A magnolia, he thought, but he could have been wrong about that.

He bent backward and rotated his hips for a moment to loosen up after a night and half a day on the big horse.

"Ridin' fah, mistuh?" a voice came from the rickety porch attached to the front of the tiny store.

Longarm turned and smiled at the stringy fellow in long johns and bib overalls. He had a graying beard that looked like he hadn't shaved since the war—the Mexican war. He was chewing on the wooden stem of a corncob pipe. He was smiling a welcome that reached his eyes and not just his lips.

"Far enough, an' got a ways to go yet," Longarm said,

still stretching to loosen some of those kinks. "You got anything t' eat in there?"

"Why, yes, I do. Why you askin'?" The smile turned into a grin.

Longarm laughed. "Neighbor, I'm so hungry I could eat a alligator if you'd hold the tail for me."

"Which shows what you don' know, mistuh. It's the tail part that's good to eat."

"Then whatever it is that you got that's eatable, I'll have some of it," Longarm said.

"C'mon in. We'll see what looks good to ya." The man motioned for Longarm to join him and went inside the shack, Longarm following, windmilling his arms and rotating his shoulders. Long rides didn't usually bother him so much, but the brown horse was thick through the barrel and Longarm's legs were not normally spread so far apart.

"Something in here smells awful good," Longarm said. It was true. There was a pot on the little woodstove that was emitting a scent that got Longarm's mouth to watering and his belly to rumbling.

"Possum stew," the fellow said. "That be all right?"

"Anything that smells that good has t' be all right," Longarm told him.

"Bowls over there in that box," the man said. "Pick you one. An' a spoon outta that seegar box on the shelf up there."

"I'm obliged," Longarm said, selecting what appeared to be the cleanest of four wooden bowls and a pewter spoon to go with it.

His host ladled up a generous portion of possum stew. The stuff was hot and peppery and tasted perhaps even better than it smelled.

"Got any grain I can buy?" Longarm asked.

The gent nodded. "I could spare you a peck or two."

"That would be fine. And something for me t' carry along as I might be sleeping far from a roof tonight. Canned milk if you got any. Jerky. Whatever seems reasonable."

"I'll put a poke o' goods together fer ya. How much can ya pay?"

"I got a couple dollars. Would that cover it?" Longarm returned.

"Cash money?"

Longarm nodded. "Paper, not specie."

The storekeeper grunted. He did not look quite so pleased with the prospect of having to take paper money, but he grunted again and then he, too, nodded.

Longarm was on his second bowl of the stew when three men came in. They looked like younger versions of the storekeeper except that these were carrying muzzle-loading rifles. Squirrel guns, Longarm thought, judging by the size of the bore of the one rifle he could see face on. The other two were being carried slanted across the men's torsos.

All three, he saw, carried their rifles with their thumbs draped over the hammers. They were ready to cock and fire should they so choose.

"Jess," the one in the lead said, nodding to the storekeeper.

"Curtis," Jess returned. "Johnny."

"Y' know what we seen outside?" Curtis asked. "We seen a mighty good-lookin' hoss. Good build on 'im. Like as not he could draw a plow good as any mule an' still look good come Sat'dy night for courtin' Annabelle Hammonds."

"Belongs to this gennelmun here," Jess said, inclining his head toward Longarm.

"Figured as much," Curtis said.

The one called Johnny, Longarm noticed, drew his thumb back, cocking his squirrel gun. Behind Johnny, the one whose name Longarm had not heard was doing the same.

Longarm smiled. "You boys looking for some trouble?"

"No trouble, mister. We jus' aim to take that there horse off you."

"It isn't for sale. It's government property." Longarm set his bowl down and turned to face the three.

Curtis's face lit up like Longarm had just given him a present. "Gov'ment proppity? Lawsy, mister, that jus' makes it all the better." His face hardened. "Now you hie on outta heah and don' give us no trouble an' maybe, jus' maybe you'll live to see tomorra."

"Boys, I got to warn you. Back the fuck off. I got business up the road and I ain't got time to mess with the likes of you. Now, scat lest you piss me off."

"Shee-it," the unnamed one in the rear sneered.

His rifle barrel started to swing in Longarm's direction. The others were in the process of cocking their weapons.

Shit indeed, Longarm thought.

His hand leaped to the grips of the Army .45, his thumb cocking the piece even before the barrel cleared leather.

The son-of-a-bitch long barrel hung up for a moment where it stuck out the bottom of Longarm's holster. The sight caught on the leather there. Or something.

Exactly what the problem was did not matter.

The third man's rifle spat smoke and flame and Longarm felt a burn across the right side of his ribs.

His vision was obscured by the smoke, but perhaps that

was a blessing because a second rifle went off—he could not see whose—that bullet passing somewhere close but not hitting its mark.

By that time he wrenched the Colt free and got into the game, firing carefully spaced shots into the cloud of white smoke. He heard cries of pain, dropped to his knees so he could see beneath the billowing smoke. Curtis was down and likely dying with a bullet in his belly.

Longarm saw a pair of legs from the knees down, adjusted his aim and shot that man, too.

The third man turned. Longarm shot at the son of a bitch anyway to make sure he would not run outside to reload and wait for Longarm to come out. That one ran off and Longarm was not sure he had hit his mark with that one.

"Jesus God," the storekeeper breathed.

"Yeah. Ain't that the truth," Longarm said.

He ran out, mounted the brown, and got the hell out of there. He was a good mile down the road before he realized he had been hit, a rifle ball passing through his right side, through and through. He felt like it had busted at least one rib on its travels.

The wound was bleeding profusely and if he did not get that hole plugged pretty damned soon there would be no point bothering as he would simply run out of blood.

As it was he was feeling kind of wobbly.

In fact he was feeling one hell of a lot wobbly.

He leaned forward over the brown's neck and gave the horse its rein.

That was the last thing he remembered.

Chapter 26

His nose itched.

That was strange because he hadn't thought anything would itch after you were dead.

So maybe . . . maybe he wasn't dead.

He felt like he was dead. Felt weightless, like he was floating.

Except that his damn nose itched.

Longarm moved his hand. Really. His hand. So maybe he wasn't dead after all. But he heard his grandmother's voice. He was pretty sure he remembered that, and she had been dead for years. Since he was a kid. Yet he thought for sure he'd heard her voice.

He tried moving his hand again and encountered something heavy and scratchy and . . . it took him some time to work it out but what he was feeling was a blanket. A very heavy, coarse blanket.

It was covering him and he was lying down. On his back. With the blanket over him.

He scratched the side of his nose then, again. It was good to be able to do that.

But he did not remember . . .

Where the hell was he and how had he gotten here?

He was lying somewhere. On a bed? He thought so.

And he was naked.

His side hurt like a son of a bitch and he was naked beneath the blanket.

He remembered—sort of—being shot.

Getting on the horse.

He did not remember very much after that.

Now he was naked. On a bed. Under a heavy, scratchy . . . he sniffed . . . rather foul-smelling blanket, rank and musky.

He scratched his nose again.

And sank back into whatever oblivion he just came from.

Chapter 27

"Wake up for me, honey. Come on now, wake up."

His grandmother's voice again. He smiled.

"I seen that. I seen you smile. Now wake up, honey."

Longarm opened his eyes, expecting to see his grandmother's wrinkled brow. Instead he saw coal-black hair around a face he never in his life saw before. She was in her fifties or thereabouts, skinny and wrinkled but most assuredly not his grandmother.

The woman smiled. "See? I knowed you was in there." She looked away and said, "Tommy, come help me here."

A man appeared above Longarm's bedside, a scrawny fellow who could have been a twin of one of those assholes who shot him, right down to the shaggy hair and bib overalls. He looked to be about thirty, perhaps a little younger.

Instead of causing harm, however, this man bent and slipped an arm gently behind Longarm's shoulders and raised him up while the old woman piled pillows behind his back. From the way the pillows crackled when he lay on them he guessed they were filled with dry corn shucks.

"There, now isn't that better?" The woman pulled a stool to the bedside, picked up a wooden bowl and pewter spoon, and began feeding him a warm, peppery broth. Lordy, it tasted good. He did not think he had ever been so hungry.

"You're lucky, mister. Couple times there I was ready to hand Tommy a shovel an' tell him to go dig your grave. You been out, let's see, this is your fourth day now. Tommy is the one as found you. Laying beside the road, you was, and a horse standing over you. You was holding onto a rein, he said. It was the horse that he seen. Saddled and everythin' an' you layin' on the ground dead to the world.

"You're luckier 'n you know. Most folks hereabouts . . . not that we have so very many as lives around here, you understand . . . but most folks would've tooken your stuff an' left you there t' die. Or killed you off t' make sure you didn't get better an' come after your stuff. But me and Tommy, we're Christian folk. Good book says not to steal, so we never. Tommy lifted you up onto that horse an' fetched you here to me. I'm a healer, I am. Best one in these parts if'n I do say so my own self. You tell him that, Tommy. You tell him."

Tommy, who did not seem to talk much if only because he could not fit a word in edgewise, nodded agreement.

"Here now," the woman said. "Drink some more o' this here broth. When he got you here an' seen you was alive Tommy got down his gun and went out into the woods. Shot one of them wild porkers that tears up my garden ever' last year no matter how I try an' build a tight fence. Tommy, he shot that hog an' dragged it home an' that there broth is the result. It's stout. Got some yarbs in't that'll help you to heal. Got you a wound in your side but that ain't what nearabout killed you. No, what done that is all the blood you lost. Tommy said your horse and gear was just sopped with it. He washed it all off o' course, an' I washed you down. Washed your clothes, too, I did. Mended the holes where you was shot. You can see where I mended, but it ain't so awful bad a job if I do say so. Now the thing is to mend you, d'you see."

Longarm looked down. The scratchy blanket had slipped down to waist level and he could see that the woman had bandaged him tight with something that looked suspiciously like she had torn up a sheet to make his bandages. He guessed that to these charitable people a genuine bedsheet would be a valued possession. They really were Christian folk, he thought, living out their faith with works and not merely words.

"Eat now, honey," the woman said, holding the spoon to his lips. "Do you get you to feeling a mite better I'll fix you some fresh side meat to go with this broth." She smiled. "That'll put the sap back in you, honey. Now eat. It's what you need."

He ate. Somewhere toward the end of the bowl his eyes drooped closed and he slept again.

Chapter 28

The next time he woke it was pitch black and silent. A mosquito—maybe a swarm of the little sons of bitches—was buzzing noisily around his face. He drew the blanket a little higher over his ears and tried to look around at his surroundings.

Soft snores came from somewhere to his left and he rolled that way, a persistent deep ache invading his torso on his right side where the bullet wound was annoying and the broken rib sharply painful whenever he breathed. Still, breathing was better than the alternative.

His eyes adjusted to the bit of moonlight that came in—along with those damned mosquitoes—through an open window.

His hosts, Tommy and the woman, were lying side by side on a pile of dry corn shucks on the bare, packed earth floor of their cabin. They did not have a blanket over them. It occurred to Longarm that he had been given the use of their only blanket. And that what was likely their only sheet was now in strips that bandaged his wound and wrapped his ribs. He felt truly touched by their kindness.

Somewhere nearby a dog yelped in fear or in pain. Tommy sat up and snapped at the dog to shut up. Which it did.

The man lay back down. And a few moments later Longarm smiled silently to himself as he heard the rhythmic rustle of the dry corn shucks crackling as Tommy had a nocturnal piece of the woman's ass.

Longarm chuckled a little. So much for his notion that the woman was Tommy's mother, never mind how much older she looked.

The sounds went on, slow and easy, for quite a long time before Tommy's breathing quickened and his thrusting became more and more rapid until Longarm could hear the man's belly slapping harder and faster against his woman's flesh.

Then there was silence again as Tommy made one last thrust with a loud grunt to finish.

One of them sighed, Longarm was not sure which, and the woman mumbled something too softly for Longarm to hear what was said.

Tommy rolled over and was snoring again within seconds. The woman lay still for a time, then rose and began building a fire in the fireplace on the side wall of the cabin.

By the light of her fire she began mixing the batter for corn cakes.

Longarm lay back with a sigh. And drifted away to sleep again.

Chapter 29

"Damnit, Custis, you ain't fit enough to ride yet. Best you stay another week with us. Let that rib set itself better. Do you get on that horse again it's gonna shake your whole innards loose."

"The animal has a pretty easy gait, Tom. I'll be all right," Longarm said. "I've been here too long as it is, takin' advantage o' your kindness."

It was almost two weeks since Tommy found him passed out beside the road. By now Anton Gardner and the redhead were surely long gone. He would have to follow a cold trail if he wanted to find them. And, oh, he *did* want to find them. Bastards!

"Really, Custis, we both think you should stay longer," Mildred Thompson put in. Tommy's actual first name was Arlen but he never used it.

Longarm smiled. "Do I lay about any longer eatin' your good cooking, Milly, I'll get fat as one o' those hogs you been feeding me. I swear, by now I must've et two porkers by my own self an' be starting in on a third."

She laughed. "Well, if you do insist on going you can

at least take some bacon with you. Tommy's got three or four sides hanging in the smokehouse."

Longarm bent down and kissed the woman's forehead. "You've done wonders for me, both of you. I don't know how I could ever thank you enough. For sure I don't know how t' repay you for all you done."

"We don't ask no payment except for knowing we done right by one o' God's flock. That and your thanks are plenty enough for us."

"You certainly have that," Longarm said, meaning it. "I'd be dead for sure otherwise an' I won't never forget either of you."

"Glad we could help," Tommy said.

"You're good folks. Both o' you," Longarm said, offering his hand to shake with Tommy and giving Milly a hug. The two of them practically felt like family after the way they took him in and cared for him. He was almost sorry to leave them.

Almost. He was champing at the bit to get after Gardner and that deceitful bitch of a woman now that he felt up to riding again.

His ribs still hurt like hell, but the wounds in his side were scabbed over where the bullet entered and then exited again, and he figured he could stand the pain of movement easier than the pain of inactivity.

Longarm gathered up the reins of the horse Tommy had been tending for him for all this time. He stepped into the saddle and shifted back and forth a bit to reacquaint himself with his seat, then touched the brim of his Stetson to the couple. He rode out of their little farmyard with a twinge of regret to be leaving them.

The horse, thank goodness, did not rock. It did shake its head a few times and twitch its ears a little but there was no display beyond that. Longarm was sure he could win any bucking contest the horse might start, but he knew his ribs would hurt like a son of a bitch to do it.

What he needed now was to get to Lake City as soon as possible. He not only needed to get back on Gardner's trail, he needed to find a telegraph and a post office—the telegraph to let Billy Vail know he was still alive and working, the post office so he could turn in a voucher in exchange for some cash.

Tommy and Milly did not know it yet, but he left every cent he had back there in their cabin. He knew they would not accept payment for taking care of him, but he had been eating their food—and much of the time even occupying their bed—and they had little enough to share, eking out a living on a hardscrabble farm.

The two scarcely had a pot to piss in, but their generosity was as boundless as their good humor, and if he could contribute a little to their larder, why, that was all to the good.

Hell, he was still wearing their only bedsheet wrapped around his body to keep that busted rib in place.

He put the old artillery horse into as fast a walk as it could manage without breaking into a bone-pounding trot and headed north on the road toward Lake City.

Chapter 30

There was not much to Lake City in the state of Florida. A few stores, two churches, a scattering of houses, and that was pretty much it. Longarm spotted a wire strung on spindly poles beside the road and followed them to a general mercantile in the center of town. He dismounted at the side of the store and tied his horse to a telegraph pole.

"Yes, sir, can I help you?" The storekeeper was a pudgy young man in sleeve garters and galluses.

"I'm a deputy United States marshal. I been robbed of my money an' my badge." He omitted mention of the money he had drawn back at Fort Marion. "I need t' send a wire to my boss back home in Denver, an' I need t' give you a gummint voucher so's I can get some cash from you. I'll need the cash an' some travelin' supplies, too, as I'm tryin' t' track an escapee."

"My," the storekeeper said, "it's a shame you weren't here two weeks ago. There was a federal deputy come by here. He got two prisoners out of our hoosegow." The young fellow winked. "Had one other prisoner with him, he did, but that one was a dandy."

Longarm groaned. "Don't tell me. The son of a bitch had a redheaded woman prisoner with him."

The storekeeper's eyes widened. "Why, however did you guess that?"

"Because the cocksucker who was showin' that badge around was flashin' *my* damn badge. He's the bastard as robbed me down by Fort Marion way, him and that treacherous woman o' his. His name is Anton Gardner and he is one murderous son of a bitch in addition to bein' a liar an' a thief."

"Oh, my. I gave him . . . that is to say, he bought . . . two horses, a mule, and supplies enough for the four of them for a week of travel."

"Shit," Longarm grumbled. "Did he say where that travel was takin' them?"

The storekeeper shook his head.

"Maybe he mentioned it someplace else in town. I'll ask around. Meantime I need t' get a wire off to my boss, U.S. Marshal William Vail in Denver, Colorado." He thought for a moment and added, "This Gardner, did he happen t' send any wires?"

"No, sorry."

"Was it you he bought the horses an' mule from?" Longarm asked.

"I sold him the mule. I had taken it in against a debt. Had it boarded down at Lew Adams's stable. That's where he saw it and the horses, too. One of them belonged to Lew and the other to Will Jefferies."

"Decent horses, was they?" Longarm asked. "I mean t' say, are they far-travelin' sort of animals or common?"

"Just middlin' these were," the storekeeper said. "Nothing special."

"All right then. Let me get that message off. I expect I'll have t' wait for an answer so's you have something official t' go by since I want t' make my purchases on the strength o' my signature on a voucher form."

"Yes. Sorry, but I think that would be best," the young man said. He gave Longarm a shrug and a wan smile. "Under the circumstances and all."

"No offense taken," Longarm said. "'Tis only sensible." He grinned and added, "An' I'll have t' ask you to trust me for the price o' the message since I don't have a lone cent on me."

"I expect I can front you that much." He hesitated. "You, uh, really are a deputy marshal?"

Longarm laughed. "Yes, I am. You been burnt once. I won't do it to you again."

"All right then." The fellow handed over a yellow message form and a stub of a pencil.

Longarm carried them to a glass-topped display case to lay the paper on so he could write out his message. Instead he gave a yelp of pleasure.

"Is something wrong?" the young man asked.

"No, sir, it's just that I see a short-barreled .45 Colt layin' on that shelf down there. You wouldn't consider swappin' it for this practically new Army model with the longer barrel, would you?"

"Even up?" the storekeeper asked, friendliness giving way to business.

"I'd go some boot with it," Longarm said. "On that same voucher, o' course."

"Let me see your gun."

Longarm handed it over and the storekeeper inspected it. The fellow returned Longarm's revolver to him and nodded. "Your pistol and tw . . . uh, three dollars on your voucher. I'll accept the voucher and work out whatever you want put on it."

"Fair enough," Longarm said. He placed the long-barreled Colt on the counter and took the short-barreled gun in exchange. He removed the cartridges from the Army model, snapped the loading gate open on the shorter weapon, and thumbed the cartridges into the cylinder.

There would be no repeat of a front sight hanging up on his holster leather, damnit. That almost got him killed the last time it happened.

He wrote out his wire for transmission all the way out to Colorado where Billy Vail could get it. Longarm handed the pencil and message form back to the young man and said, "It might take a while t' get an answer. Where's that stable so's I can go talk to the livery man while I'm waiting t' hear back from Billy?"

The storekeeper gave him directions and bent over his telegraph key. Longarm listened for only a moment to satisfy himself that the young fellow knew what he was doing with a key, then went out to find that liveryman who sold Gardner his horses.

Chapter 31

"Sure, I remember him," the blond, dirty-faced liveryman said. The fellow winked. "I remember his prisoner even better."

"Yeah, right," Longarm said dispiritedly. "Good-looking redhead female."

"You know her then, you being a federal man your own self," the liveryman said.

"Oh, yeah, I know her."

"What did she do?" the liveryman asked.

"Robbery," Longarm told him. It was the truth. He knew since he was the one who had been robbed. "I understand he took some prisoners from here."

"Not from here like as if they was local boys. These was strangers. I don't know who but Clive Marcum could tell you about them."

Longarm lifted an eyebrow.

"Clive, he's our constable. Handles the law local-like, and he's a deputy for Sheriff Burch. The sheriff is away. He's over to Jacksonville doing who the hell knows what. I know because he rented a buggy from me to make the trip." The man snickered. "Went without his fat wife, I know that, too. Not that I blame him. If I was married to that woman, I'd go on trips without her any time I could. Hell, if I was married to her I'd shoot myself. Or her."

Longarm laughed. "I know the type. Tell me about the horses, please."

The man shrugged. "Ordinary five-dollar ponies is all. Both of them seal brown and plain. Pencil necks. Kinda scrawny all over. They wouldn't win no races, either one of them. Now, the mule, it was pretty nice. Black with a pale muzzle and a brand, FR Connected, on the left hip. The horses wasn't branded, neither one of them."

"Is that usual around here?" Longarm asked.

"Yeah, pretty much so. We don't have much crime of any sort, certainly no horse stealing. Besides, everybody pretty much knows everybody else's livestock so there wouldn't be no sense trying to steal something."

"You sold him saddles?"

The fellow nodded. "Couple old Spanish saddles. Cuban, I'd suppose. They got those dinner-plate saddle horns and wide fenders. Now that I think on it, it'd be easier to recognize the saddles than those horses."

"Thanks, friend. You been a big help. One more thing. Did they say where they was headed?"

"No, sir, they did not. If anything, they was kind of secretive about it. But I got the impression . . . and mind now, I'm not exactly sure how I happen to think that way . . . I got the impression they was heading someplace south."

"But someplace in particular?" Longarm asked.

"Oh, yes. I'd say they was going someplace in particular."

"All right then, thanks. Now where can I find this Constable Marcum?"

Chapter 32

"Mister, I personally know Deputy U.S. Marshal Long and you ain't him." Constable Marcum seemed to harbor no doubts about that. His stare was hard and his jaw firmly set.

And what a jaw it was. Longarm was sure he had seen houses smaller than Clive Marcum. The man had arms the size of most men's legs, black hair, a ruddy complexion, and a three-day growth of beard so black his face looked almost blue. He had bright blue eyes and long, curly eyelashes that a woman would give her left tit for. The blue eyes, however, did not make the man look angelic. Far from it. He looked like a brawler, an impression that was reinforced by the puny little nickel-plated revolver on his belt. Irish, Longarm guessed, and not afraid to use the nightstick carried loosely in his left hand.

"You got it wrong, Constable. The man you met as me, which is to say as Deputy Long, is Anton Gardner. You probably have paper on him. Him and his gang are murderers an' robbers. Crafty sons o' bitches. They show up an' strike every once in a while. Reason I'm after him is

to take Gardner back to Denver for trial. Him and his boys
robbed a U.S. Army payroll a while back. Fella name of
Craig over along the coast caught him an' turned him in
at Fort Marion. I come down from Colorado t' fetch him
back where we can put him permanent behind bars. He
got away from me . . . my own damn fault for not payin'
attention to that redheaded woman who seems t' be in on
things with the man . . . an' now I'm tryin' to make up for
my stupidity. If you doubt me, wire Fort Marion an' ask
for descriptions o' me and of Gardner, too. That should set
you straight about who's who."

"And I am gonna do just that, mister. Meantime you
can set in a jail cell here."

"Like hell," Longarm snapped.

Marcum did not argue the point. He merely stepped in
close until his belt buckle was pressed hard against Longarm's shirt front. His left hand took a grip around Longarm's
right bicep so hard it felt like he was being squeezed by a
steel band. With his right hand Marcum snagged Longarm's
Colt out of the leather.

He tossed the revolver onto the sheriff's desk and picked
Longarm up as easily as if he were a child's rag doll.

"This way, please," he said, smiling, as he carried Longarm bodily to the back of the room and into the lone cell
back there.

Marcum deposited Longarm onto the wooden bench
that was the only piece of furniture in the iron-barred cell,
turned, and left.

The cell door clanging shut sounded god-awful loud,
Longarm thought.

He sighed. The big man had not searched him so he
still had his .41-caliber derringer. But what the hell good
that would do he did not know.

Looking at Clive Marcum, Longarm got the impression that if he did shoot the constable the bullet would only bounce off the man. And anyway Longarm had no desire to harm him. Marcum was a fellow peace officer doing what he perceived to be his duty.

He was wrong about what he thought, of course, but he was acting the way a good lawman should. Nail the suspect down until the facts could be established. Better to apologize afterward than to be bamboozled a second time.

Inwardly grumbling, Longarm sat on the damned bench and pulled one of his last cheroots from his inside coat pocket.

Chapter 33

Longarm was lying on the bench—hard son of a bitch it was, too—when he heard the door open. The front door, not his cell door unfortunately.

"Wake up, you." It was Marcum's voice. Longarm did not bother to open his eyes or turn his head to look at the man. "Supper time. Sit up."

Longarm yawned. Was it that late? Apparently. He sat up and paid attention.

Sunlight no longer streamed through the windows and the shadows had grown deeper.

Clive Marcum stood beside the cell door with the large key in hand. Behind him was a girl, eighteen or nineteen years old or thereabouts. She was blond and buxom and would have been pretty except for a severe overbite and consequent buckteeth. She was barefoot and wore a plain, gray cotton shift, a costume that seemed to be the norm among the poor in this part of the South.

The girl was carrying a tin pie plate covered with what looked like an old dish towel. She had a spoon in one hand and a napkin clutched in the other. The napkin, oddly, had been starched and ironed, a fact that seemed out of place under the circumstances.

"You want to eat?" Marcum asked.

"Sure, I could eat."

"Stand to the back of the cell then."

Longarm complied and the girl, who had not spoken a word except with her eyes—which were large and brown and surrounded by laugh lines—handed the plate to Marcum.

The deputy opened the cell door and swung it open. He entered the cell, obviously not at all concerned that the prisoner might make a grab for his pistol. Longarm could easily have done that, but he suspected Marcum would be able to beat him to death with one swipe of his enormous paw before Longarm or any prisoner would have time to accomplish anything with a weapon as puny as a firearm. Marcum was obviously confident in his strength. And probably with very good reason.

Longarm took the heavily laden plate from him and sat on the bench. "Thanks. The, uh, spoon an' napkin, please?"

"Oh. Right." Marcum left the door standing open while he turned back to the girl and took the articles from her. He gave those to Longarm, stepped out of the door, and this time carefully locked it behind him, going so far as to take hold of the bars and rattle them to assure himself that the door was secure.

"You'd best leave now, Kristy," the big deputy said. "I got to go finish making my rounds."

"Can't I stay till the killer is done with my plate and spoon, Clivey? Please? Pretty please?"

Clivey? Longarm shook his head in amazement. Who the hell would have thought?

"Sure, if you want to. Just stay far away from the bars, far enough that he can't reach out and grab you."

The girl's eyes went wide. "Do you think he would really do that, Clivey?"

The deputy shrugged. "Who knows. But it could happen. Don't let it."

"Whatever you say, honey."

"All right then." Marcum turned his attention back to Longarm. "You in there, Long. Or whoever you really are. Don't you be giving this young'un any trouble or you'll answer to me for it."

Longarm nodded and pulled the towel off his supper plate. His nose wrinkled in distaste. The contents of the plate seemed to be a gray-brown mess of . . . something. Mashed potatoes. He was fairly sure that was the basis for it all. Potatoes with bits of this and that thrown in. It looked awful. But the smell, well, that was plenty good enough.

Marcum left and Longarm took a tentative bite. The stuff was delicious.

"What the hell is this, girl?"

She laughed. "Do you like it?"

"Yeah. It's terrific."

"I mix it up myself. There's gravy and peas and all sorts of stuff. The crunchy bits are Jerusalem artichoke. You really like it?"

"I do," he assured her.

She stepped close to the bars, taking hold of two of the vertical rods and hanging on them with her face pushed between them.

"Didn't the deputy tell you to stand clear o' the cell?" Longarm said.

The girl grinned. "I don't do everything I'm told. Do you?"

"I don't reckon anybody does. Not really." He took another heaping spoonful of her concoction and encountered some of the crisp, crunchy pieces of Jerusalem artichoke.

Her eyelashes fluttered a little, not deliberately he thought, and she said, "Are you really a killer?"

"I'm really a deputy United States marshal, but Deputy Marcum doesn't seem t' believe me when I tell him that."

"But have you killed people?"

"When I've had to."

"Have you ever killed a woman?"

"Now what in the world does that have t' do with anything?"

"Have you?"

He sighed. "Maybe. Couple times. When I've had to."

He could see some color rising in her cheeks and spreading onto her forehead, and her breathing quickened. "Are you what folks would call a dangerous man?" she asked.

"I reckon so. Some might, anyway."

"Could I . . . could I touch you? Please?"

"Hard t' do from the other side o' the room, which is where Marcum told you t' be."

"But I'm right here. Right . . . oh!" She wriggled her hips and gasped for breath, and he could almost believe that she was having an orgasm just from the thought of being with a dangerous man-killer. "Come here for a minute. Please."

"What if the deputy comes back?"

"He won't," she said. "He'll be gone at least a half hour walking the town like he does every evening at this time and then he'll stop at the café for his supper, and I'd say it will be at least an hour before he gets back. So will you please come over here?" She laughed. "I won't hurt you. I promise."

Longarm shrugged and set the plate down on the bench at his side. "Sure, why not."

He stepped over to the bars. The girl reached through and unerringly took hold of his dick through the cloth of his trousers. Her eyes widened again. "So big."

"You don't quit messin' with it an' it's gonna get bigger."

She giggled. "Let me see."

"No, damnit. Let go."

"Oh, pooh. Let me see." She began unbuttoning his fly.

He could have put a halt to this by simply stepping back away from the cell bars. But he did not. He stood there while the girl unbuttoned his britches, reached inside, and pulled out his cock, which by then was standing tall and near about to burst.

"It's pretty," she enthused. "It isn't just big, it's awful pretty." She began rubbing the shaft up and down, expertly peeling back his foreskin and looking him over. "It's clean, too. Guys that have the clap, you can see some pus or whatever right there at the tip. But you're clean. Do you have crabs or anything?"

"Now that's a mighty odd question for a pretty girl t' ask," Longarm said.

She looked up and chuckled. "Do you really think I'm pretty?"

Longarm nodded solemnly and lied, "Yes, I do."

The girl dropped down to her knees and tugged him closer. "No, closer than that," she instructed. "Hold yourself right up tight ag'in the bars."

He did and she pushed her face close to the cell while pulling him—selected parts of him anyway—through to her side. She licked his cock all over and ran her tongue around the head, then took him into her mouth.

The feel of her was warm and eager as she applied suction hard enough to pull a corncob through a keyhole.

"Ahh! Oh, jeez." Longarm took a firm hold on the cell bars, hanging on with both hands while the girl—it took him a moment to recall what Marcum had called her—while Kristy gave him a slobberingly wet blow job. She made snuffling, gobbling noises as she sucked, holding on to his shaft with one hand and tickling the flat behind his balls with the other, her mouth engulfing him and then pulling back against the power of her own suction before she rammed forward once more.

It was a feeling Longarm could have enjoyed by the hour, but he was amazingly horny, perhaps because of the oddity of the setting, and he found himself all too quickly building to a powerful climax.

Kristy continued to suck even after his jism exploded into her mouth. She swallowed everything he had to give and tried to pull even more out.

When at last she allowed him to withdraw she looked up and laughed, rubbing her forehead where a red mark had appeared. "These iron bars are kind of hard, you know? I bonked my head ag'in them pretty hard. But it was fun. Thanks, mister."

"Shouldn't I be the one t' be thankin' you?"

"Only if you liked it."

"Oh, I liked it just fine. I can promise you that." And this was no lie.

"Go ahead and finish your dinner now, mister killer. I got to take that plate back or Miz Heatherton will be getting after me."

He smiled. "We wouldn't want that, would we?" He returned to the bench and picked up his plate and spoon once again.

The girl giggled. "I hope you're in here tomorra night still."

"I don't." He smiled again. "Well, except for that one reason."

"You really liked it?"

"Uh-huh," he said around a mouthful of the tasty mess.

"You really think I'm pretty?"

"Uh-huh."

She seemed delighted, even if she did have to press him for the compliment.

If a man had to be in a jail cell, Longarm thought, this one might not be the worst.

Chapter 34

Longarm did not have the very best night he could remember. The bench was harder than rocks and the mosquitoes were as big as Rocky Mountain quail. Or anyway the bloodthirsty little bastards sounded that big as they buzzed around his ears. By morning he was a patchwork quilt of lumps and itches.

He did get through the night, however. Breakfasted on another plate of the delicious mess brought by Kristy—but no blow job this time—and spent half the morning staring at the back of Clive Marcum's head as the big deputy sat hunched over the sheriff's desk.

Sometime late in the morning a boy came in, a lanky kid of twelve or fourteen wearing homespun overalls and apparently nothing else. He was barefoot and bareheaded but seemed cheerful enough. He was carrying a pair of yellow papers.

"Telegram for Constable Marcum," he announced, "and one for Deputy Marshal Long."

Marcum jerked upright in his chair. "Marshal Long, you said, Tommy?"

The boy peered down at the papers, shuffled the one on
the bottom onto the top, and read aloud, "Deputy United
States Marshal Custis Long. That's who it's addressed to,
Constable."

"All right. Let me see it." Marcum held his hand out to
receive the papers but the boy, Tommy, shook his head. "I
can only give you yours, sir. It's against the rules for me
to give this other'n to anybody but Deputy Long."

Marcum grumbled but inclined his head toward the cell
at the back of the room. Tommy handed Marcum his message and brought the other back to Longarm.

"Sorry I don't have no money on me, son. You deserve
a tip."

"That's all right, sir. I understand."

Marcum made no mention of a tip for the boy. After
taking a moment to stare at the firearms resting in a rack
against the side wall, Tommy left.

Longarm tore open his message. It was signed William
Vail but very likely was sent by Henry in Billy's name.

ASSUMED YOU DECEASED **STOP** PLEASED TO BE
CORRECTED ABOUT THIS **STOP** ALREADY ISSUED
NATIONWIDE ALERT FOR GARDNER AND COMPAN-
IONS **STOP** AUTHORIZING DISBURSEMENT OF ADDI-
TIONAL TRAVEL FUNDS **STOP** RETURN DENVER
IMMEDIATELY END OF MESSAGE S/ VAIL COMMA
U S MARSHAL

"D'you want t' see this, Marcum?" Longarm asked,
holding the message form out between the cell bars.

The constable rose from the desk and shook his head.
"No need for that, Long. This wire from the major down
to Fort Marion sets the record straight. He says the man I

met before is Gardner and you're the real federal man. Sorry about that." He fetched a key ring from his desk drawer and came to unlock the cell door and swing it wide.

"You were doing the right thing, Marcum. I know that. Hell, I would've done the same myself."

"Can I make it up to you with a few beers and a look at Sydney's free lunch spread?" Marcum offered.

Longarm grinned. "As one lawman to another, I'd be proud t' hoist a few with you, Clive."

Marcum offered his hand and Longarm gladly took it.

"I'm buying," the Lake City constable said.

"That's good," Longarm laughed, "because I won't have a penny to my name till I get over to the post office an' cash a voucher."

Marcum clapped him on the back and guided him out the door and into the next block where an apron-wearing bartender named Sydney was pouring schooners of quite excellent beer and providing a free lunch spread that was not too terribly fly-specked.

Chapter 35

As soon as he left Marcum, propped up on the brass rail at Sydney's saloon, Longarm headed for the post office. He badly needed some cash in his pockets. For one thing he felt as sticky as if he had been dipped in mucilage; he just was not accustomed to the heat and humidity down here. And did not want to hang around until he did get used to it.

"I thought you'd be by soon," the pudgy clerk said.

Longarm raised an eyebrow and the clerk laughed. "I'm the one took that wire for you, you know. I know what it said."

"Oh, right. I forgot."

"How much do you want on that voucher?"

"How much can I get?"

The clerk shrugged. "Up to, oh, a hundred, maybe. I expect the Yankee government is good for it."

"Now I know good an' well you're too young to 've served in that scrape."

"True, but my papa and my uncles did. You?"

"Yeah, I reckon."

"Which side, if you don't mind me asking."

"Does it matter?" Longarm asked.

"No, I expect not. Not this long after. Anyway, do you want the hundred?"

"Sure."

The young man took a cigar box out from under the counter, opened it, and counted out $96.40 in cash, which he pushed across the glass to Longarm. "I took out for the difference on that pistol swap and for the telegraph message. Is that all right?"

"Just fine," Longarm said. "Two more things if I may. No, three. One, I want t' buy some underbritches an' a new shirt. Two, I want you t' guide me to a barber. An' three, where can I find the kid that brought my message form over to the jail?"

"The boy will likely be hanging around the barbershop. It's where I generally find him when I want something, which means they're both right around the corner in this same block. Over that way." He pointed. "The balbriggans and shirts are over here."

The young man led the way.

An hour later Longarm felt like a completely new man, shaved and bathed and wearing clean clothing. He also felt better about tracking down the kid and giving him a dime, a little more than usual because the boy had been so cheerful about *not* getting a tip before.

Longarm headed for the café for a lunch of fried chicken, mashed sweet potatoes, and field peas, then back to the mercantile.

"What can I do for you now, Marshal?"

"I'm needin' some supplies to take on the road. Flour, coffee, jerky if you got any. Seegars. An' cartridges for my .45 and for that old scattergun I picked up on my way up here. Single-ought buck if you got any."

"Twelve gauge?"

Longarm nodded.

"I can fix you up."

"Oh, yes. Almost forgot. I'll be needin' some gun oil. Whale oil is best. D'you carry it?"

"I do. Over this way." He took a small can of sweet oil down from a shelf and asked, "How long do you want to provision for?"

"Call it a week. I expect I can find another place to restock in that time if need be."

"Give me a half hour. I'll have everything ready for you when you come back."

"Thanks." Longarm went back to Sydney's place. The beer was just as good this time, especially when he used it to chase a shot of rye whiskey. He limited himself to two, then headed for the livery to fetch his horse. It was time to get on the road.

Chapter 36

"Gardner didn't say anything t' give you a hint about where they was going?" Longarm asked.

The town constable and part-time deputy sheriff shook his head. "No, they didn't, and I didn't ask." Marcum lifted his mug and drained it, then slapped it down onto the bar with a bang. Apparently he had been drinking steadily since Longarm left him two hours earlier. Now he seemed to be feeling the effects of the alcohol.

"Did you notice which way they went when they pulled out?" Longarm asked. The brown horse was tied in front of Sydney's saloon, already saddled and loaded with a burlap sack full of provisions.

"Nope," Marcum said.

"I did," the bartender put in.

Longarm raised an eyebrow.

"The man I thought was a deputy marshal came in here to buy a pint of brandy. I watched him when he left, him and the redhead." Sydney grinned. "Maybe I was watching her more than him. Point is the four of them, the marshal and the woman and the two prisoners, they rode out down that way." He pointed toward the south end of town.

"Could have been a ruse," Marcum said. "I think it was." He slurred his words just a little. If the man was not drunk, he was well on his way toward it.

The bartender shrugged and turned away from the conversation to wipe some already clean glassware rather than argue that opinion.

"Could have been," Longarm agreed aloud. But he did not believe Marcum was leading his little troupe on a false trail. There was no reason for him to do such a thing as at the time the whole town believed he was a deputy United States marshal. He had been under no suspicion here.

In fact, Longarm mused, the man acted like he was perfectly comfortable down in this distant corner of the South. Acted like this was his home place. Or close to it.

"South, you said," Longarm said aloud.

The bartender nodded without turning away from his stack of mugs and bottles.

"Thanks." Longarm ignored the constable, who seemed not to notice anyway. Marcum at this point was holding on to the bar to keep from weaving.

Longarm touched the brim of his Stetson to Sydney and went outside. He paused to light one of the panatelas he had gotten from the mercantile—rolled farther south in Tampa, the clerk had said, by Cuban workmen who knew cigars—then untied the brown and stepped into the saddle.

South it would be.

"Yeh, I seed dem," the old black man said emphatically. He turned his head and spat. "Got water from my well, dey did. Den dey didn' even thank me. Said sumpin over dey shoulder 'bout lazy niggers, I s'pose 'cause I settin' on dis porch wid a broken leg. Den dey get back on dey horses an' ride on."

"Which way?" Longarm asked.

The old man pointed with his cane. "Dat way."

South, Longarm thought with a nod. Always south. Gardner and his gang had someplace to go down there. Someplace where they felt safe between their forays to rob and kill.

"May I have some o' your water for me and my horse?" Longarm asked.

"Hep yo'sef. De good Lord gibs de water free fo' all His creatures, mistah man. I don' nevah charge fo' my water."

"Thank you, sir." Longarm dropped the moss-covered oak bucket into the old man's well, waited a moment for it to fill, then pulled it up. He drank of the sweet, pure water, then offered the rest to the brown, which drank noisily, splashing water over the side of the bucket and blowing snot.

Longarm threw aside the quart or so that remained and turned to ask, "Can I draw some for you?"

"I could use some o' dat, mistah man. It be hard fo' me to do nowadays."

Longarm pulled up another bucket and poured it into a pail that he set on the old man's porch. The fellow smiled and said, "You wants t' know where dey be goin' now?"

"That's right. I'm looking for them," Longarm told him.

The old fellow cackled and said, "Nobody pays no mind to a ole nigger. Thinks we don' hear nothing or we too stupid to unnerstand what dey say. Ha! I hear dat man ask de woman how far dey gots to go. She say dey be dere two, three day more."

"Did she say where that would be?" Longarm asked, his interest quickened now.

The old man shook his head. "No, sah, I'm sorry."

Longarm grunted. Two, possibly three days farther south. Tampa, where the cigars were made? Possibly. The distance would be about right if he understood correctly.

Thinking of cigars, he pulled out one of the excellent panatelas and lighted it, then brought out a fresh one which he offered to the old man on the porch of his shack.

"Why, thankee, young fellah." He smiled, showing an incomplete set of yellowing teeth. "Dey say somethin' mo'. Somethin' 'bout cow critters. The woman, she de one talk about de cows."

Longarm's brow knitted in a frown. Cows? Where the hell would they be finding cows in the middle of fucking Florida?

He struck a match and lighted the old boy's smoke, shook it out, and thanked him for the information. Then he returned to the saddle and pointed the big brown horse south. Always south.

Chapter 37

It took a while for Longarm to recognize the source of the discomfort that had been nagging at him ever since . . . he had to think about that for a while. Ever since he crossed the Mississippi or soon after.

The problem was that he could not *see* the way he usually did.

Oh, there was nothing wrong with his vision. That was as sharp as ever.

But the trees. The damnable trees. Sons of bitches were everywhere. Crowding a man. Practically closing in on him.

At home in the mountains and on the plains, a man could stand in his stirrups and see to the end of forever.

Here in the southland he was lucky if he could see for an unobstructed fifty, sixty yards.

Big trees, little trees, thick underbrush, strange growths, gray moss draped over all of it . . . it all cut into a man's vision and made him feel surrounded, positively hemmed in by all that greenery.

No wonder the Seminole Wars had lasted so long and

been so very ugly. The damned Indians could be hiding unseen and unsuspected when they were within hatchet striking distance.

That would have been a hell of a way to fight a war, Longarm thought. He was glad there was no more of it now. It was bad enough knowing that jungle creatures, things he did not know and could scarcely imagine, might be lurking nearby. The idea of fighting men in this terrain would have been even worse.

He stopped at a nameless village along the sandy track leading southward and bought a chunk of ham still warm from the oven and a pan of cooked field peas to go with it. Then, fortified, he rode on for another half hour until he found a narrow creek half hidden beneath a canopy of wild grape vines, the fruits hard and green.

Longarm stepped down from the brown and kicked around in the grass to satisfy himself that no snakes were hiding there, unsaddled, and assembled the makings for a small fire.

He did not need to cook anything as he was still full from the meal of ham and peas, but he wanted the comfort of a fire to sleep by.

He dipped a can of the slow-moving brown water out of the creek and boiled a pint or so of coffee, which he enjoyed along with a cigar.

He did not have a bedroll so he spread his saddle blanket on top of some of the bunched grass and lay down.

As dusk turned to night he draped his coat over his face to ward off the swarming mosquitoes. Somewhere in the night a panther screeched, followed by noises that were foreign to him. As far as a westerner might know those sounds could have been made by anything from monkeys to unicorns and he would be none the wiser.

As he dropped into sleep he was thinking, south, Anton Gardner was moving always south.

The problem was, there was a hell of a lot of "south" down there where the bastard might be.

Chapter 38

Longarm woke to a world of hurt. A world of itch would be more accurate. The mosquito bites on his face and arms were bad enough, but the ones that damn near drove him crazy were the bites on his knuckles. Those, close to the bone as they were, seemed even worse than bites on his meatier parts. And to make matters all the worse, at some point during the night he seemed to have been assaulted by an army of the impossible-to-see little sons of bitches they called chiggers.

Those had found their way into his britches and were burrowing into his crotch. That itch was even worse than the ones on his knuckles. Far worse.

He tried riding on toward the south but found he was itching so bad in his crotch that it was all he could do to stay in the saddle. Well before noon he came to one of the many small rivers that laced the landscape here.

Fuck it, he told himself. Anton Gardner would just have to wait for an extra half hour or so.

He dismounted and unsaddled, then hobbled the brown and turned it loose to graze along the sandy, oak-shaded riverbank. He turned the saddle blanket upside down and spread it in the sunshine to bake, that being the most effective way to eliminate tiny varmints.

He did the same with his clothing and for the same reason, draping one piece at a time over the taller weeds and grasses out away from the trees that lined the river bank. He even turned his hat over and set it under the sun.

When all of that was accomplished and he could at least hope for a more comfortable situation as soon as the sunshine did its work, Longarm stepped into the cool, slowly moving black water of the shallow river.

He sighed.

Such wonderful relief!

He was comfortable for the first time since he woke that morning. The water bathed away all the itching and discomfort left behind by the damnable bugs and cooled him from the moist, oppressive heat.

Longarm lay back on the tannin-stained verge of the river, closed his eyes, and let his lower body float while his shoulders and head maintained a light contact with the earth. He felt weightless and almost disconnected from the harsh realities of the day.

He was convinced this was the most comfortable he had been since he got on that train back in Denver. And wasn't that a hell of a long way from here.

He was . . .

"Damn, you have a big dick."

It was a girl's voice and it came from not very far away. From not far *enough* away.

Longarm's eyes snapped open and he jerked upright. Pushing deeper into the water, he turned to see whoever it was who spoke.

The woman was probably in her twenties with long

black hair. She was thin enough to be stringy, as so many of the poorer people were down here. They looked like it was all they could do to eke out a meager existence from land that was nothing but sand and jungle. She had bad teeth and a mottled complexion.

She blinked. "You really do have a big dick, mister. Stand up outta that water so's I can get a better look at it."

"Like hell," Longarm shot back. "Go away."

She giggled. "No, I want to see."

"I'm gonna stay right here until you leave," Longarm told her.

"Are you sure 'bout that?" She pointed downriver from where Longarm had entered the stream. He looked, fairly sure she was trying to pull his leg somehow but looking despite that conviction. There was a moving V on the placid river surface. Whatever it was it was swimming toward him. Moving fairly quickly, too.

"What the . . . ?"

"Gator," the girl said. "There's a nest of 'em close by. My pa traps one ever' now and then. The tail tastes pretty good an' we tan the hides for leather and sell them. Don't get much for them but it's something. I think that's the old bull gator. I seen him take down a full-grown mule once. Good mule, too. Pa got so mad he almost shot the old boy then. Would have 'cept he sires so many young'uns that Pa almost thinks of him as part of our livestock. Kind of like that old rooster that pecks the littler kids but he don't go into the pot 'cause he covers the hens so good."

"The, uh, alligator . . . would he really . . . ?"

"You suit yourself, mister, but was I you I'd be gettin' out o' that water right about now."

The gator was a dozen yards away and still swimming toward him.

Damn thing really was an alligator, too. He could see the two eyes protruding slightly above the water surface, their gaze as cold and evil as that of a rattlesnake.

"Shit!" Longarm yelped as he came bursting out of the river.

He grabbed for the Colt that lay close by on the bank.

"Don't shoot him," the girl shouted. "Damn, mister, don't shoot him or my pa will be awful upset."

Longarm was so concerned about the approach of the alligator that for a moment he forgot that he was standing bare-ass naked with a strange woman not twenty feet distant.

She grinned. "Yep. You really do have you a powerful dick there, mister. It's a real whopper."

She approached him, reached down and touched his cold, limp pecker. Longarm reacted involuntarily, his cock beginning to thicken and lengthen as she peeled his foreskin back. She flicked the tip of her little finger back and forth across his piss hole and laughed when he stood tall and firm.

"Shy, aren't you," Longarm drawled.

She looked up at him and in a completely serious tone said, "Not so's you'd notice it, mister."

"Y'know, I kind of suspected that," he said.

Her expression did not change when she said, "I'd admire to feel that thing inside me."

Custis Long was nonplussed. What the hell do you say to a complete stranger who walks up, takes hold of your private parts, and then says something crazy like that?

Chapter 39

Maybe if the woman had been better-looking, Longarm mused as he rode away, he would have taken her up on the offer. As it was, all he wanted was to get dressed and saddled and the hell out of there.

Interesting folks they had down here, though, he was thinking. Not much like home.

He rode into a sunbaked village that had a signpost erected at the outskirts, presumably what they considered to be the town limits, that read Alachua. He had no idea how somebody would pronounce a word like that. Likely Seminole, he suspected.

Licia probably would have been able to tell him. Damn shame it was that crazy woman back by the river he ran into instead of a sweet little gal like Licia.

Thinking of Licia . . . and of the way it felt when the dark-haired girl took hold of his pecker . . . he began to get horny. Rocking back and forth on the saddle did nothing to alleviate the condition.

He found a store. Of sorts. It was not much of a store, selling mostly moth-eaten clothes that looked like they had been picked out of a rag bag somewhere, but it did have some alligator jerky.

Longarm winced as he thought about his own treasured dick and balls becoming food for that bull gator back there. The mere thought of it hurt and he shriveled up smaller than he had probably been since he was in grade school.

"Couple pounds of that jerky," he told the proprietor, who was one of the few fat men he had seen since leaving St. Augustine.

The man turned his head and spat into a rusting tin can. "Stuff comes dear," he mumbled. "Cost you ten cent a pound."

"I'll take two pounds," Longarm said.

"You got cash money?"

"Yes, sir, I do."

The fellow took the bag of jerky to the end of the counter where a set of scales sat. He weighed out what passed for two pounds. Longarm pretended not to notice the cheating bastard kept a wayward thumb on the scale while he was doing it.

"I'm tryin' to find some friends o' mine," Longarm said as he dug into his pocket for twenty cents. "They might've come this way, oh, a couple weeks back or thereabouts."

"What's their names?" the fat man asked, pulling a faded blue kerchief from the front of his bib overalls and mopping some of the sweat that was running off his forehead.

"My friend is Anton. Calls himself Andy sometimes," Longarm said, improvising details he did not know. "Last name is Gardner. I don't know the names of the folks he's traveling with but one o' them is a redheaded woman. Quite a looker, that one is."

"Oh, hell yes. I remember them. Them passed through about the time you said. On their way south but in no hurry about it. They stopped to eat at my auntie's house. She puts out a good table, I must say." He laughed. "She's the reason I got to looking like I do." His hands fluttered, sketching his own large belly and triple chins. "Yeah, they surely did pass this way. Damn good-looking woman."

Longarm nodded. "That'd be them, all right. Did they happen t' mention where they'd be going from here?"

"Sorry, no. Why are you looking for them?"

"I have a message for my friend Andy. Private message sort of thing so I can't be telling you what it is."

"Oh, hell, I don't mind that." The man laughed again. "Nobody ever tells me anything anyhow."

"Now why don't I believe any such of a thing," Longarm said, suspecting that this fellow had big ears and could repeat three-fourths of the gossip that flew through the town. "Where'd you say this aunt of yours lives?"

The big fellow gave directions to a rickety, sunbaked house near the south edge of the community. The place was of the kind they used to build in rural Texas, two cabins with a covered dogtrot between them and a chimney on each end.

Longarm approached an older woman, gray haired and sweaty, who was bending over a huge kettle behind her place, stirring whatever was in there with a paddle big enough to row a boat with.

He gave the kettle an inquiring sniff. The odors coming off it did nothing to encourage an appetite.

The woman noticed what he was doing and laughed, her laughter sounding much like that of her nephew. "This is my laundry I'm b'ilin' here, sonny."

Longarm chuckled. "In that case I feel some better about this. Sammy over to the store said I might get a cooked meal from you."

She nodded. "Twenty cents. You got cash?"

The nephew had asked the same. He was beginning to get the impression that there was not a hell of a lot of available cash in this community. "I do, ma'am."

"Then set you down at the table here and I'll fill your belly for you." Which she did, with fatback and black-eyed peas, sweet corn still on the cob, and mashed yams drenched in molasses. Longarm felt a hell of a lot better when he rode away from there three-quarters of an hour later.

South. Always to the south.

Chapter 40

"Sure, I 'member 'em." A nearly toothless grin flashed. "Truth is, I don't remember much about them fellas. But the woman?" The farmer rolled his eyes. "I sure as hell remember her. The four of 'em stopped at Widow Peak's house. Spent the night there an' pulled out midmornin' that nex' day."

"Where could I find this widow lady?" Longarm asked.

The farmer gave directions to a place not a quarter of a mile distant. Longarm followed a dusty lane through a grove of orange trees, the blossoms laying a candy-sweet scent on the air.

Widow Peak lived in a two-story cracker-box house, severely upright and unadorned with not even an overhang above the front door to relieve the square contours nor were there any plantings around it to soften its appearance. The house was plain, weather-grayed cypress. It was a no-nonsense sort of place.

A line of wash hung drying on one side. On the other and set back to the rear was a shed containing stacked boxes, each box flat, perhaps two feet by three and a foot deep. Beside the shed sat a heavy farm wagon and a light buckboard. There surely had to be horses or mules to pull those vehicles but Longarm could neither see nor hear any.

There was no provision for hitching visiting animals so Longarm dismounted and hobbled the brown. He mounted the squared logs that served as steps and rapped on the front door. Moments later it was opened by a lady wearing not the drab and shapeless things most women here seemed to adopt but a flowing gown of pale blue with a tight-fitting, low-cut bodice showing the pale tops of some very attractive breasts while below her waist the gown was wide, riding on either a set of hoops or starched crinolines.

The gown was lovely but more appropriate for a gala than for the late afternoon of an ordinary weekday.

Above the softness of those pale tits things were not quite so attractive.

The woman was on the shady side of thirty. Hell, she was probably in her forties. She wore too much face powder and her lips were artificially red. Her hair was a glossy brown done up in a tight bun and her eyes were a very bright blue, almost the same shade as her gown but very bright.

"May I help you?" Her voice was soft. She did not smile.

Longarm swept his hat off and introduced himself.

"A United States marshal, you say? How odd. You are the second such I have received of late."

"Actually, ma'am, if you're speaking of a man named Anton Gardner and his traveling party, he wasn't no marshal. He was my prisoner. He escaped with the help o' that woman traveling with him and he's been representing himself as a deputy every since. Misrepresenting, I should say."

"May I see your badge, please?"

"No, ma'am, Gardner stole it. But I do have a telegram

from my boss back home in Denver, Colorado. I could show you that if you like."

"Please do. But first come inside. We can have tea while I look at your document."

"Yes, ma'am."

Longarm remembered to carefully wipe his feet before he entered the widow's home.

Chapter 41

"Yes, Mr. Long, I do upon occasion accept boarders." She blushed. "I don't wish to be crude but . . . have you cash to pay for your lodging?"

"Yes, ma'am, I do." It was not yet dark and he could make another five or six miles before he needed to find a place to camp for the night, but he considered there was a very good chance the lady might have overheard some comment from the foursome about where they were headed.

"A . . . a dollar?" She sounded as if that were a very great amount of money, so much that she was not sure she should ask it.

Longarm nodded. "A dollar will be fine, ma'am. An' for my horse?"

"Another dollar? Would that be all right?"

"Just fine, ma'am."

The lady straightened her shoulders and lifted her chin, the crass but very necessary subject of business having been gotten out of the way now. "I have a barn behind the house. You can put your animal there. There is hay in the bunk and millet in a bin. You should find everything. If not, come get me and I will see to things. And you may call me Mrs. Peak." She managed a small smile. It made her much more attractive although she was in fact not a pretty woman.

"I'm sure everything will be fine, ma'am." Longarm smiled and donned his Stetson and went back outside. He led the horse around to the rear of the house and found the barn set about fifty yards away. Its four stalls held two tall, rather handsome mules, which brayed unhappily when Longarm brought his horse in and turned it into a stall. He removed his tack and draped it over the wall of the remaining empty stall. He put the sweaty blanket upside down on top of the saddle so the blanket could dry.

He climbed a rickety ladder and tossed down hay for the brown, found the grain and poured a gallon for the brown to munch. The horse was not being hard used but needed more than just hay for the constant travel.

He took a few minutes to rub the horse down with a square of burlap that he spotted among the usual debris found in almost every barn, then he picked up his saddlebags and returned to the house, this time tapping on the back door.

Again the lady answered quickly. "Come in, Mr. Long. Are you hungry?"

"I could eat."

"Go on through to the parlor. Help yourself to a seat and I shall join you shortly."

He started toward the front of the house, but she stopped him as he reached the kitchen doorway. "Please do not smoke inside the house," she said. "Nor in your room tonight."

"Yes'm," he said.

He was not sure where to put his saddlebags since Mrs. Peak had not yet assigned him a bedroom so he carried them with him and dropped them onto the floor beside the plush upholstered armchair he found in the dark and rather gloomy parlor.

The chair was comfortable and he would have wagered that it once was the dead husband's. He pulled a leather hassock in front of it and rather gratefully put his feet up, resting his boots on the hassock and instinctively reaching for a cigar. Then he remembered. He was just too damned comfortable to get up and go outside for a smoke. Later, he thought. Later would be soon enough.

Longarm put his head back and closed his eyes. This was the most comfortable he had been since . . . hell, since leaving Denver actually.

He could hear Mrs. Peak doing something in the kitchen. The sounds were homey and relaxing, and if he was not careful, he would sleep right through whatever meal she was working on.

Chapter 42

"Mr. Long? Wake up, Mr. Long. Supper is ready."

He woke slowly, slightly confused at first. His head ached and his belly was rumbling. Night showed outside the parlor windows and a pair of lamps were burning. He had no idea when she might have done that. "Mrs. Peak," he said aloud.

"Yes?"

"Oh, I . . . just remindin' myself. For a bit there I clean forgot where I am."

She smiled. "You must be very tired."

"Yes, ma'am. More than I knowed." He yawned. "Been on the road a bit, you see."

"Is that other man really not a deputy?" she asked.

"He really ain't."

For some reason the lady blushed. Then shook her head very slightly. "Will you go after him?" she asked.

"Yes'm. Just as far an' as hard as I got to."

"What will you do if you catch him?"

Longarm grinned. "The question ain't 'if', it's 'when.'"

"My apologies," she said with a smile.

"Did you say something about dinner, ma'am?" he reminded.

"Supper. Yes."

Of course, he thought. In the South, dinner was the major meal of the day, coming in midday. At night it was supper, a much lighter meal. Habit prompted him to pick up his hat and carry it with him to the table, but he left the saddlebags in the parlor.

Mrs. Peak had the table covered with freshly starched white linen, the places set with crystal and bone china. There were so many forks and spoons in so many different sizes that he did not know what the hell to reach for first.

"May I pour, Mr. Long, or would you prefer to do that?"

"You have the honor, ma'am."

She nodded. "As you wish." She took a tall, brown bottle out of a silver bucket. There was no ice to be had, but she used the bucket anyway. "This is a scuppernong, Mr. Long. Very pleasant, I think. It comes from our own grapes."

He held his glass while she poured. Longarm was not much of a wine drinker, but he wanted to be polite. He tasted the stuff. It was pale and sweet and fruity, but he figured he could wash that taste away with a belt from the bottle of rye in his saddlebags.

Supper—not dinner, damnit, supper—was roasted chicken, baked sweet potatoes, field peas, and biscuits so light and fluffy you had to pour some gravy over them to keep them from floating off the plate.

"Ma'am, this is the finest meal I've had since I left home, an' that's been a lot o' years back." That was not the literal truth but a little flattery never hurt anyone.

She beamed. "You really like it?"

"Yes, ma'am, I most surely do. Best I've had in ages."
As if to prove his point he took another biscuit off the plate.

"Here. Butter it, Mr. Long, and pour some honey over it." She smiled. "Trust me, it will be good."

Biscuits and honey. Turned out the combination was better than merely good. He had another. Then a third. Chicken and peas he could get pretty much anywhere, but biscuits like these were few and far between.

"I do like to see a gentleman appreciate my cooking," Mrs. Peak said as Longarm was surrounding his fourth biscuit.

"Ever'body likes t' be appreciated," he said between bites.

"That is so true," she enthused. "Would you like more wine?"

"No, thanks, ma'am. I'm happy with the water here."

"I shall serve coffee after our meal, of course," she said.

"Of course." He did not much see how she could manage coffee on top of all the wine she was knocking back. He had only taken a meager sip from his glass but she was quickly coming to the bottom of the bottle. He was not sure, but the lady was beginning to sway from side to side on her chair, and he suspected she was becoming more than a little tipsy.

"It's been a long day," he said after the meal. "If you don't mind, ma'am, I'll turn in now. If you'd just show me to my room . . . ?"

She gathered her skirts and with a rustle of crinolines rose. Longarm remembered barely in time to jump up and assist her with her chair.

"This way, please."

He hurried into the parlor, grabbed his saddlebags, and followed her up a steep, unlighted flight of stairs.

Chapter 43

Longarm padded barefoot down the stairs, found the kitchen in the dark, and pumped a pitcher of water that he carried back up to his room so he could sponge some of the day's sweat away. He had stripped down and was in the process of cleansing himself when he heard a loud crash and, moments later, a plaintive "Mr. Loooong."

"Shit," he mumbled aloud. He hurriedly grabbed his britches and pulled them on, then went to rescue the lady from whatever distress she had gotten herself into.

"Mr. Looong? Mr. Long!"

He followed the sound of her voice to a closed door down the hallway from his room, shrugged, and tried the knob. The door swung open.

Mrs. Peak lay on the floor, naked from the waist up, her legs—limbs, he supposed she would prefer that they be called—tangled in a sea of ruffled crinolines. She was on her back, flopping around like a turtle turned upside down.

"Help me, Mr. Long."

He tried to hide a laugh at seeing her predicament.

What he did not laugh at was her tits. So pale they

glowed silver in the moonlight coming through her wide-open window, they were simply magnificent. Big as pillows with large, dark areolae surrounding nipples that were nearly as large, and as prominent, as Longarm's thumbs.

Her waist was smaller than he would have suspected, and her hair was down. Probably she had toppled over and fallen while in the process of brushing her hair before retiring for the night.

"Help me," she repeated.

"Yes, ma'am."

He went to her side, bent, and scooped her up into his arms. She was a substantial woman and he had to strain a little to get her up. Mrs. Peak slipped one arm behind his neck to help support herself. That put their faces close together and before he knew what she intended, Mrs. Peak's tongue was in his mouth.

Her other arm came around him and the widow's kiss intensified. She began to moan softly.

And he began to suspect that the lady was not nearly so drunk as she wanted him to think that she was. The wine was but an excuse for letting go of the restraints imposed by a rigid society.

That was fine with Longarm. His cock hardened as he felt the passion in her kisses.

He placed her down on the big four-poster bed that dominated the bedroom. He noticed that she had no difficulty slipping out of the crinolines once she was on the bed. He shucked his britches and lay down beside her.

Mrs. Peak reached for him eagerly, grabbing at his cock, gasping with pleasure at the size of it, her tongue hot and wet and probing into his mouth.

Longarm took hold of one of those magnificent tits. It

was soft, almost fluid beneath his fingers. The nipple on top of it was rock hard. This woman was hungry to feel a man's penetration between her legs.

She pulled him on top of her without waiting for any foreplay. She deftly guided him into her cunt, hot and dripping with juices too long unspent.

She made low, grunting sounds and wrapped her arms and legs alike tight around his body, clutching him to her, into her, demanding that he fuck her.

"Long," she whispered throatily, "So good," and he was flattered until she added, "So very long." It was not Custis Long she meant then but how long a time it had been since she felt a man's cock invaded her pussy.

Her body pumped and writhed and it was all Longarm could do to keep up with her frantic movement.

He felt her go rigid and her arms tightened around him like steel bands as she reached a climax within a minute or so of that frenetic coupling.

Longarm made no attempt to catch up with her orgasm. There would be time enough for that.

He waited until she went limp beneath him, then gently withdrew. He gave the lady a moment for her breathing to return to normal, then kissed her softly and guided her head down to his still-rigid cock.

She took him into her mouth, tasting him, licking her own juices from his shaft, peeling his foreskin back and running her tongue around and around the head, sliding him in and out of her mouth, sucking harder and harder until he exploded into her mouth.

Mrs. Peak continued to suck, swallowing his come and cupping his balls in her hand.

"Now," he said finally, "now that we've both taken the

edge off, let's us do some slow an' serious fucking, shall we?"

The lady looked up at him from between his legs. And smiled.

Chapter 44

Longarm woke staring up at the ruffled canopy over Mrs. Peak's four-poster. He yawned and stretched. The truth was that he was feeling rested now and better than he had felt in quite some time.

The lady stirred at his side. She was smiling when she awakened and opened her eyes to see him there beside her.

"Good morning." He kissed her, and she rolled onto her side and pressed her body against his. He immediately got a hard-on—another hard-on, that is; there had been a number of them during the night—and slid inside her.

Mrs. Peak nuzzled his neck while he filled her body, rocking her to a powerful orgasm. Longarm's release quickly followed, then the two lay together, he still inside her body.

"Are you hungry?" she asked.

He chuckled. "Not if it means I gotta come out o' you. I'm enjoying just layin' here like this."

She kissed him and sighed. "Can you stay?" she asked. "Can't you stay with me for a while? A month? At least a week? It has been so long for me and it is good to have a man in my bed again."

"Y'know, from the way you acted yesterday, the way you blushed at one point there, I kinda got the idea you'd been with Gardner when him and his gang stopped here."

She blushed quite furiously at his words. "How did you know . . . ?"

"Readin' people is a big part o' what I do," he told her. "Tell me about Gardner. Do you mind?"

"Oh, I mind all right. I was foolish. And I thought he was a deputy marshal, don't forget. I thought he was a good man. Instead he used me. The next morning that bitch sniffed and tossed her head and said he told her I wasn't nearly as good as she was. She said he would have been in her bed except she was having her monthly."

"She was bein' jealous," Longarm said. "That's all it was."

Mrs. Peak sighed. "I suppose so, but it hurt."

"O' course it did. What's the woman's name, anyway? That's something I can't recall ever rightly hearing."

"Her name is Amanda. Amanda Chesterton. That isn't the name she was using when she was here, but it happens to be her real name. I know that. I've seen her before though she didn't remember the occasion."

Longarm sat up. "You know her?"

"I know her family. She is the last of the family line, I believe. The last survivor. The Chestertons used to be a powerful family. They practically ruled the center of this state as their own fiefdom. They had cattle by the thousands. Timberlands. Orange groves. Then like most of us they were ruined by the war. There was no fighting this far south, but we were ruined nonetheless, my family as well as hers. I've heard talk that Amanda is reclaiming the Chesterton fortunes somehow."

Longarm snorted. "Reckon I know how."

Mrs. Peak raised an eyebrow.

"Gardner has been on a tear. Robbing an' killing. Him and his gang have took plenty in the way of loot from all they done. Now I'm beginning to think they've been helping this Amanda Chesterton rebuild what they lost. I dunno. Maybe Gardner and her intend t' run that part o' the state. Maybe they want t' be the powerhouse. Do you happen t' know where they was headed then?"

"Oh, of course I do. Not that they admitted to it. In fact they said they were on their way to Cuba, but I know better than that lie. They've been saying that just to throw off any ideas people might have, but Amanda Chesterton . . . or Gardner, as she might be now . . . would never so much as think about abandoning her heritage."

She blushed again. "I was going to tell you about them anyway. I mean . . . it has nothing to do with last night. And this morning. And . . . this." She pulled away a little so that his cock slid out of her, then she bent down to take him in her mouth again.

Mrs. Peak was a lusty one, all right.

Not that Longarm minded.

He smiled as she continued to suck his cock. He really should ask what her first name was.

Chapter 45

Carldene. That was her name. Carldene Fahrqua Peak. Nice lady. Longarm felt considerably refreshed as he rode away from what remained of the Peak estate.

South. Again south.

But now he knew why. And where.

He bumped the brown horse into a trot, even tried it at a lope now and then, but the heavy-bodied artillery horse was no pleasure at its choppy lope and was even worse at a canter. It moved just fine at a trot though and could hold that gait damn near the clock around, or so it felt beneath him. The truth was that he had become rather fond of the big old thing and would regret having to return it to the army once he was ready to go back to Denver where he belonged.

He nooned beside a slow-moving, dark water stream, dining on a sack lunch that Carldene packed for him and getting lost not more than half a dozen times in the maze of sandy tracks that wound their way through what looked more like jungle than forest, around cypress bogs and impenetrable palmetto stands, then opening up briefly to lush clearings green with tall grasses.

Hogs and cattle ranged wherever they damn pleased and if any of them were branded or earmarked, he could not see it from the wary distance they maintained from him. He supposed the folks hereabouts could work out who owned what. Or not. Hell, as far as he knew these livestock might be regarded as community property and rounded up whenever and by whomever was needed.

He knew a great many cattle were shipped from Florida to Cuba while a good bit of tobacco and leather products returned in the other direction.

Damn, but it was hot though. Hot and sticky and uncomfortable to someone accustomed to the crisp mountain air and the clean prairie winds of the West. Longarm would be beyond glad to get back to Colorado.

With any kind of luck he would be on his way back there soon enough.

All he had to do was find Anton Gardner and put the son of a bitch back in irons where he belonged. In irons. And then in a hangman's noose for that long and final drop.

At the thought of Gardner being brought to his final justice, Longarm nudged the brown from a walk back into a trot.

South. Always south.

Chapter 46

"You wouldn't happen to have any cheroots, would you?" Longarm asked the one-armed storekeeper.

The lean, gray-haired old man shook his head. "No cheroots but I have some pretty good blunts. Would those do?"

"Reckon they'll have to. I smoked the last o' what I had this forenoon."

"How many?"

"Half a dollars' worth," Longarm told him.

The old fellow opened the lid of a humidor and grabbed out a handful, placed them on the counter and separated a dozen of the plump cigars, which he pushed across the counter to Longarm. He returned the rest to his humidor, accepted the fifty-cent piece Longarm gave him and put the coin into a leather bag under the counter.

Longarm nodded to the empty side of the man's body, where an arm should have been. "What happened, if you don't mind me asking?"

The storekeeper grunted. "You're probably wondering did I lose this in the War for Southern Rights. Well, I did.

And I didn't. I was in the army at the time. In Pickett's brigade, I was. The one you hear about, the boys who made that grand charge at Gettysburg. I wasn't with them that day and I've always thought that maybe losing this arm saved my life because of it.

"Truth is, me and one of my messmates caught us one of some Pennsylvania farmer's chickens. I was gutting the son of a bitch and nicked myself with my own knife. The cut turned bad and the army sawbones took my arm off because of it. That's the reason I wasn't there beside my comrades that day. They was shot to hell and all my best and dearest friends died that awful day while I laid useless in the tent that passed for a hospital." The old man looked close to tears.

Not that Longarm blamed him. He'd seen close friends of his own go under.

The storekeeper sighed and wistfully said, "I would have given more than just an arm for our glorious cause. I almost wish I could say that I had."

"I understand," Longarm lied. He coughed into his fist and asked, "The Chesterton ranch. Do you know it?"

"Oh, hell yes. Everybody in this part of the state knows of Duke Chesterton."

"Duke? The only Chesterton I've heard of is Amanda," Longarm said.

"Amanda is the daughter. Duke was the he-coon for thirty miles in any direction. But he died, oh, three or four years ago. Big doings at the time. Men in silk hats and solid-gold watch chains came from all over the state for that funeral, let me tell you. Folks talked about practically nothing else for months after."

Three or four years. If Longarm remembered correctly, that was about how long Gardner and his gang had been robbing and killing, but the sons of bitches had been smart enough to avoid committing any federal crimes until they hit that army payroll up near Fort Caspar. It was an interesting coincidence. If indeed it was a coincidence.

What was it that Carldene Peak said? The Chesterton fortunes had faded but now Amanda was returning them to their former glory. With stolen money, it seemed, and the blood of innocents.

"Can you tell me how t' get down there?" Longarm asked.

"Oh, hell yes. You just go out here and down this track . . ."

Longarm carried his purchases out to the brown, secured the cigars in his saddlebags, and stepped back into the saddle. He gathered up the reins and pulled the brown's head around.

Toward the south. Always south.

But not much farther now.

Chapter 47

"Sure, mister. Everybody around here knew Duke. Real cracker, that man. The real thing."

Longarm was puzzled. "A cracker? I thought . . ."

The fellow laughed. "You thought a cracker is a poor man, didn't you. And so it would be up in Georgia. Up there a cracker is a shellcracker. Someone so poor he has to get along by picking up shells along the shore and eating them. Down here a cracker is a whip-cracker. A man on a horse who uses a whip to handle his cattle or his dogs. Or his nigras. Yeah, everybody knew Duke. Of course now Duke's place is being run by his daughter Amanda." The gentleman winked. "Quite a looker, that one."

"Yes, I've had the pleasure o' meeting her," Longarm said. "Goin' out to her place t' see her now." He smiled. "Or anyway I will if you can tell me the way to her place."

"Easy as pie. You take the road out to the east, see, and then . . ."

Longarm thanked the gent and returned to the brown. There was a public watering trough in front of the county courthouse. He led the horse to it and pumped fresh water

into the hollowed-out cypress trunk, then let the horse have
its fill before mounting again.

It was late in the afternoon, late enough that he could
have delayed going after Gardner and the woman. He could
have turned to the local law for assistance, too. He did
neither. He was anxious to get this little matter disposed
of. And he did not know how a request to put the county's
leading citizens in irons would be viewed by whoever rep-
resented law and order in this county.

He rode the last few miles at a walk. He wanted to reach
the Chesterton estate late enough that the residents should
be at the house for their supper rather than out working
somewhere in the pastures or the woodlots or the groves.

Lamplight showed in the downstairs windows when he
followed the lane past a rather smelly piggery and a row
of chicken coops into the well-groomed yard.

The Chesterton house was bigger than a good many
hotels Longarm had stayed in. It was a two-story affair set
about two feet off the ground by way of a row of pilings.
A porch ran around all sides, or at least the three sides
Longarm could readily see, and the very high roof suggested there was a generous attic as well, allowing air to
pass above and below the living quarters.

A small balcony on the second floor indicated either a
hallway or master bedroom up there.

A pair of oil lamps burned on either side of the broad
front steps to welcome guests.

Somehow Longarm did not think the lady of the house
would be welcoming him into her home.

He pulled up by the steps and turned to secure the reins
to a hitching post beside the steps, but before he could do
that a scrawny Negro boy came dashing around the side
of the house to take the reins from him.

"Will you be stayin' long, sir? Do you want for me to put your fine horse into a stall while you visit?"

"No, I won't be staying," Longarm said. "I don't figure t' be here long at all. Is the mistress home? And Mr. Gardner?"

"They both in the house, sir."

"And the other gentlemen?"

"No, sir, they alone tonight."

"All right, thanks." Longarm wondered if he should tip the kid, decided against it. He took a deep breath, then touched the grips of his .45 to make sure it was positioned where he liked it and that it was loose in the leather.

Then he mounted the steps and crossed the wide porch to the front door.

Chapter 48

Common courtesy demanded that Longarm knock and announce himself. But this was not a common visit and he did not feel particularly courteous.

He took his .45 out, flipped open the loading gate, dropped a sixth cartridge into the cylinder, and closed the loading gate again. He kept the Colt in hand when he tried the doorknob. The door was unlocked. He pushed it open and walked inside, through the vestibule, and into a large foyer.

Somewhere to his right he could hear the clatter of tableware and a hum of low conversation. He could smell the rich odors of roasted meat and freshly baked bread in addition to the sharper scents of new paint.

Amanda had the house spiffed up to a fare-thee-well, with new rugs and lamps burning from every wall. Hell, no wonder she needed all the money Gardner could steal if she was going to burn whale oil by the barrel.

Walking softly on the Oriental rugs, Longarm followed the sounds of dinner, past an ornately furnished parlor to the dining room beyond it.

Amanda Chesterton sat at the far end of a huge mahogany

table. Lighted chandeliers burned above both ends of the table, reflecting bright off silver china and silver place settings, and a candelabra with eight tapers contributed even more light.

Amanda's rapt attention was on Anton Gardner, who sat close by her right hand. Gardner was leaning forward, intent on some tale he was telling her. His left hand was on her wrist. His right held a silver fork that had a piece of meat on its tines.

The two looked thick as the thieves that they were.

Gardner came to the punch line of whatever story he was telling and Amanda began to laugh.

The laugh died stillborn when she looked up to see Custis Long standing in the doorway.

The handsome woman turned pale.

"Darling, what is it? What's wrong?" Gardner asked, clutching her hand with his.

Amanda nodded in Longarm's direction, and Gardner turned to see.

"Shit!" he barked.

"Anton Gardner, you are under arrest," Longarm intoned. "Again."

"No. You can't," Amanda shouted at him. "You'll ruin everything."

"You're right about that, lady. I'm ruining it all for you. Now the both o' you stand up, nice an' quiet, and turn around, wrists behind you."

"*No!*" Amanda screamed. She reached across the corner of the table and snatched the revolver out of Gardner's holster. Grasping it in both hands, she got a shot off. The virtually unaimed bullet smashed into the chandelier at the far end of the big table, sending flaming whale oil down onto the starched linen tablecloth.

Longarm reacted without thought, certainly without concerns of chivalry. Someone fired at him. Instinctively he shot back. His bullet hit Amanda in the throat and she was flung back into her elegant Chippendale chair. No doubt she would have regarded it as quite a genteel place to die.

Blood poured from her, spilling onto Gardner, who gave a groan of despair and reached for his . . . lover? Partner? Boss? Longarm did not know what their relationship might have been. Nor did he care.

He cared greatly, though, when Gardner picked up the Colt that Amanda had just taken from him.

Moving with deliberate care, the murderer turned the gun toward Longarm.

Gardner had to know what the tall lawman's response would be. Perhaps it was a form of suicide that he preferred over waiting for a hangman's rope. Whatever his reasons, he took the .45 in hand and turned it toward Longarm.

By then the tablecloth caught fire and a sheet of flame rose between Longarm and Gardner.

Gardner ducked to his right, trying to see around the fire to find his target. Longarm could see just fine from where he was. And bullets pay no heed to fire.

Anton Gardner died with Longarm's bullet in his brain. His arms flew wide, the revolver leaving his hand and thudding hard against a polished sideboard, shattering glassware stacked there.

Longarm took a long look to make sure both Amanda and Anton were indeed dead. Then he strode outside until he could be sure the whole house was not going to catch fire from the conflagration now reaching almost ceiling high atop the dining room table.

"I'm having a hard time adjusting to the idea that old Duke's daughter could have been all you say she was," Sheriff Troy Roach said with a shake of his graying head.

"It's all true," Longarm told him. "That an' more." He pointed to the steel safe they had found in Duke Chesterton's office. "You'll see that this silver gets to the nearest federal agency? It's from an army payroll and it belongs to the government."

Roach nodded. "I will, Marshal. That would be the navy. They have a detachment over to Tampa. What about you though? Won't you stay for the inquest?"

Longarm shook his head. "I been gone more'n long enough. I sent my boss a wire this mornin' saying I'm on my way back. Figure I'll catch a ship goin' to N'Orleans or Galveston. Whatever I can find. Then by rail from there, maybe. I should be back in Denver within a week or two."

"What about the other gang members?"

"I don't know who they are. If you can smoke 'em out, they're all yours."

"Any rewards attached to them?" Roach asked, a sly look creeping into his expression.

Longarm nodded. "Likely. Tell you what, when I get back t' Denver I'll check on that an' let you know."

Roach grunted, and Longarm decided the other gang members, whoever they might be, were already known to the local sheriff. And now could be considered as good as in the bag.

Longarm extended his hand to the sheriff. "Thanks for your help."

"Glad to be of service."

Longarm turned away. He mounted the big brown and reined it away. West, this time. West, toward home several thousand miles distant.

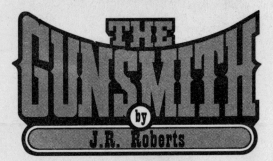
M11G0610